D1525070

THE DARK SIDE
OF THE
FIRE

RUBEN ELUSTONDO

THE DARK SIDE OF THE FIRE

This book is a work of fiction. The characters, names, incidents, dialogue, and plot are the product of the author's imagination or are used fictitiously. Any resemblance to actual persons or events is purely coincidental.

Copyright @ 2021 by Ruben Elustondo

All rights reserved. No part of this book may be reproduced or transmitted in any form or by any means without written permission from the author.

ISBN: 9798511218663

Imprint: Independently published

Acknowledgments

TURNING AN IDEA into a fiction story is complicated, and a book can't be written without the help of a lot of people. Clarity of the plot, the believability of the characters, conflicts, tension to create engagement, a credible flow, and a satisfying conclusion are just some key elements that require feedback and advice. This is achieved with the support of a team behind the author that deserves recognition. My wife Mirta, always providing guidance, suggestions, and being unconditionally on my side, and my children Andrea and Daniel, with their encouragement to pursue this literary adventure, gave me the strength to continue writing and now publishing my second novel. Special thanks to Ray and Maureen Miller for their thorough review of the manuscript and recommendations and Margaret Prieto's valuable input and insights. I can't avoid mentioning my editor, Stephanie De Arman, for her many contributions to enhance the story.

I have enjoyed writing my first novel last year and decided to continue this path of creating fiction stories with elements taken from observations and experiences. Corruption, greed, and self-interest are part of the world, as well as integrity, love, family, and friendship. When those behaviors, values, and feelings interact, conflicts emerge, and lives change. I hope this story engages you by going through the character's struggle between good and evil, relationships and individual goals, love versus friendship.

Chapter 1

THE DRIVER OF the black Suburban had been waiting right before sunrise near the address given to him close to Discovery Park. Brian came out of the high rise and went down the stairs at the front of the building. He stretched and then started his daily jog with a slow pace for two blocks until he entered the sidewalk surrounding the park. He didn't notice the car following him, waiting patiently like a big cat for the right time to attack.

The driver casually smoked with the windows halfway down, pretending to be one of those early risers who enjoyed a slow ride before getting into a dull day at the office. When nobody else was close enough to intervene, he gripped the wheel and accelerated.

Brian enjoyed the rhythm of his shoes pounding on the wet pavement and was excited about the progress he had made. He was eager to share what he had found the day before with his closest friends, Josh and Matt.

Finally, we have something. Suddenly, he heard a car engine too close, and when he turned, he felt the impact on his side. His body went airborne, bouncing off the car's hood and landing in the middle of the road amid the sounds of broken bones, stinging pain in his chest, and a warm flow coming out of his body. He didn't notice the car speeding away on that misty morning.

"Is HE GOING to be okay?" a weeping teenager asked.

"Are you family of Brian Oliver?"

"Yes, his sister, Beth. Please let me know that he's going to be okay."

The doctor had a sad expression on his face and invited her to sit down. "He was involved in a hit-and-run and was brought to the hospital. We're still running some tests. He suffered a concussion, some lacerations, a broken leg, and a couple of broken ribs."

"Is he awake?"

"He opened his eyes and seemed to have a problem recognizing people. It's normal after suffering such a shock. Our main concern right now is possible internal bleeding, and that's why we're performing a thoracoscopy."

She started crying again, and the doctor put his hands onto her shoulders, looking her in the eyes.

"We're going to do our best, and you have to have faith that your brother will get better. I'll come back as soon as we have the results of the procedure and a better understanding of his situation."

"Can I see him, please?" she pleaded.

"I can give you just one minute. Maybe seeing you will help."

Beth went into the ICU and couldn't believe that her brother, always smiling and full of life, was there amid wires and bandages. She got closer, touched his arm, and he squinted his eyes.

"Beth, love you" was barely audible.

She forced a smile. "You'll be okay," she said and squeezed Brian's hand.

"Tell Matt," he mumbled and made an effort to say something else, *"the fire,"* and then he fell unconscious.

Beth left the ICU and sat in the waiting room, looking at the floor with her head between her hands.

"Beth," two young men ran from the elevator, calling her name. "What happened? How is Brian?"

"Josh, Matt, I'm so glad you're here." She hugged them while tears rolled down her cheeks.

"Of course, we're here. Brian is like a brother to us. You're his only family around, but you can count on us as if we were family, too, for whatever you need."

The girl calmed down a little. "He was hit by a car while jogging this morning. There were no witnesses, and the driver ran away." The two friends exchanged a glance, and she continued, "A passerby found him and called the police, but the person didn't see what happened."

They remained silent for a while until the doctor came back and stared at Beth. "I'm afraid we don't have good news," his forehead furrowed. "We found that the fractured ends of the left fourth, fifth, and sixth ribs had penetrated the posterior wall of the thoracic aorta, producing what is called an aortic dissection. We need to repair it immediately with open-heart surgery."

"Oh no." Beth put her hands over her mouth.

"How serious is it? Will he recover?" Matt asked while Josh froze and stared with wide eyes and raised eyebrows.

"He's lost a lot of blood, but until we do the surgery, we won't know whether other internal organs have been affected. I'm sorry, he's in critical condition and being moved to the OR right now."

Beth slumped in a chair, Josh beat the wall with clenched fists, and Matt ran his hands through his hair while walking in circles. They didn't say a word for a few minutes until Matt stared at Josh.

"Do you think this was an accident?"

"That's what it looks like."

"Isn't it a coincidence that Brian wanted to talk

to us about something significant he had just found concerning DB Corp. and then got into this *accident*?"

"I don't know what you're thinking but be careful about what you say," he whispered while he moved his head in Beth's direction.

She was still sitting with her eyes closed. She opened her eyes and looked at them. "Brian said something strange."

Matt got closer to Beth. "What was it?"

"He said *tell Matt the fire.* Does it mean anything to you?"

He tilted his head and shrugged. "The fire? Nothing comes to mind. Josh, let's think about it and discuss it later."

It was already late afternoon when the doctor came back. "We were able to repair his aorta, but there's some damage to his kidneys. He's still in critical condition and very weak. It was a complicated surgery. I'm sorry I can't give you better news."

"Are you saying he doesn't have much chance of survival?" Josh's breathing quickened.

"Let's say that medicine has done its best, and now he's in divine hands."

Beth hugged Josh while he stroked her hair.

Matt blew out his cheeks. "He's going to be okay. He's going to be okay," he repeated with clenched fists.

THE MORNING NEWS covered the hit-and-run accident suffered by a pedestrian. *"At six-thirty this morning, while jogging on the side road of Discovery Park, a thirty-four-year-old man was hit by a car that left the scene. A passerby found the victim and called the police, who took him to St. Michael's Hospital. After going through surgery, the individual died due to kidney failure and heart complications. The police ask citizens to report through Crime Stoppers any information that could lead to the identification and arrest of anyone involved in this horrible incident."*

TWO MONTHS LATER, a small crowd of tired but enthusiastic skiers gathered at Mountain Café located across the gondola station of Crystal Mountain. It was the usual ritual after enjoying the slopes all day, where all would share stories about their skiing adventures.

Jessica put her cup of hot chocolate on the table and asked her friends, "Have you seen Matt?"

"I think he just went up for the last run of the afternoon," said one of them.

"Yes, I saw him taking the last ride on the gondola," added Josh.

Jessica shook her head. "He always enjoys the last run of the day. It's like a ritual. We've been here for hours, but he still has to go up one more time because he feels that coming down the mountain when almost everybody's gone gives him peace of mind."

"He's an excellent skier and prefers to avoid the crowds. He likes the routine; you should know that by now." Josh smiled. "And by the way, congratulations on your wedding. I heard it's coming in six months?"

Her eyes glowed. "It certainly is, but don't say anything because our parents don't know yet."

Matt and Jessica had been dating for two years, and now they felt it was time to consolidate their relationship. She had met him at this same café when she had returned from law school with her degree and dreams about a career as her parents expected. She'd had a job waiting for her at her dad's firm, Morris, Dalton, and Associates. Matt was a high school teacher at Lakeview, a private school catering to the wealthy and powerful, and was passionate about environmental and social causes. Both loved children, so they were planning to start a family soon. Jessica would postpone her professional career for a few years and stay home. Then maybe return to practice law once the kids were school age.

"There he is." Josh pointed to the last skier coming down the slope.

Matt was coming downhill fast and, at the last minute, bent his knees and slid sideways, coming to a perfect stop in front of them. "Hi, guys."

"Having fun?" Jessica grinned.

"Yes," he took off his helmet, "you know I like the late run."

"Then here's a reward for that good run." She kissed him softly on the lips and then looked at his eyes. "Don't tell me you're still worried about tonight's dinner at my parent's house."

"You know they don't like me, and every time I go, it feels like an inquisition."

"C'mon. That's not true, and I'll be there to protect you." Jessica smiled and kissed him again.

"Yes, baby. Don't cry." Josh looked at him with mocking eyes.

Matt couldn't hide his anger. "You know, sometimes you can be an idiot."

"Well, at least it's just sometimes. If this is one of those times, don't copy me and smile at your girlfriend. You're lucky to have her."

Matt didn't respond because he knew his friend was right. Why worry so much when Jessica was in love with him? On the other hand, Matt resented Josh a little because he and Jessica had an early romance in their senior year of high school, and Matt thought his friend still had feelings for her. However, his main concern was Jessica's parents. Behind their kindness, he felt some rejection due to their different social status.

THE DALTONS' HOME was an impressive river-view mansion built in a gated neighborhood in the city's wealthiest part. Matt drove his old Toyota to the gate and announced his name with some hesitation. He was given access and was parking in the circular driveway when Jessica came running out the front door. She hugged him as soon as he opened the car door and looked at his eyes with a big smile. "Are we going to tell them today?"

"We'll see how it goes."

"Matt Hernandez. Don't be a coward," she admonished him.

"It's not a question of being a coward. It's just that I don't know how they will treat me today. We don't want to tell if the mood isn't the right one."

"Aww, don't be afraid, and let's go inside. My parents are waiting for you." She caught him by the arm. Jessica's smile gave him some reassurance.

John and Mary Dalton were well-established members of the wealthy circles of the country. He was a famous lawyer, and she was the heiress of a hotel chain empire with worldwide operations. Jessica was their only child, and they had great expectations for her future, including the person who would eventually marry her and get part of their fortune. That night they had prepared a surprise.

"Good evening, Matt." John gave him a handshake while holding a glass of scotch in his left hand. "Do you want a drink?"

"Hello, John. Not right now. Thank you." They

approached the white leather sofa where Mary was just glancing through a magazine. "Good evening, Mary. Thank you for inviting me tonight."

"Nice seeing you, Matt. Glad you came." She forced a smile to her face.

"Mom, do you know that the school is planning to name Matt department head?" Jessica proudly said.

Mary's eyebrows raised. "Oh, that's great. That's certainly something I'm sure you have worked hard for, Matt."

"Thanks, Mary, but it's not confirmed yet. The principal wants to inform the school board first."

Jessica's eyes clouded with emotion. "He's so modest."

"Okay," John began walking toward the double crystal door that led to the dining room, "let's not get so emotional and enjoy a nice dinner."

"Wait," Mary interrupted, "remember we have one more guest. He should be here any minute now."

The young couple exchanged a sad look. Jessica and Matt had thought the four of them would be alone and they would be able to share their good news, but now it could get somewhat complicated.

Jessica tried to hide her disappointment. "And who's the guest, Mom?"

"You'll see in a few minutes. It's a nice surprise, and you're going to like it."

John came back and sat beside his wife with his

smiling face gone. "Let's wait then. Please, have a seat."

They were chatting for a few minutes when the doorbell rang, and the maid announced, "Mr. Morris is here."

Mary got up quickly and rushed to greet the visitor. "Tyler, we're so glad you could make it."

Tyler Morris was the son of John's partner, and he had grown up with Jessica. "Good to see you, Mary. You look as young as ever. How are you, John?" Then he shifted his attention to Jessica. "There you are. Always beautiful. I've been counting the hours to seeing you again."

Jessica smiled and introduced Matt. "Nice seeing you, Tyler. Let me introduce my boyfriend, Matt."

Tyler's smile faded a little while shaking his hand. "Good meeting you, Matt."

"Now that we're all here, let's go to the dining room." Mary motioned, and they sat around the magnificent table under the imposing crystal chandelier.

THEY ENJOYED A delicious hot crab-and-artichoke appetizer while talking about some trivial topics until Mary looked at Tyler and asked, "We heard that you've been working at a big law firm in New York after graduating from law school. Are you planning to continue your career there?"

"That was the original plan," he smiled at Jessica, "but I've decided to come back here."

"And why is that?" asked Matt, visibly disturbed. "Why would you leave a successful career in New York?"

"There are other things besides a good career," Tyler said, still glancing at Jessica.

"I don't blame you for considering other factors besides a good job." Mary smiled.

"How about asking for the main course to be served." John tried to ease the conversation into a different topic. "I heard the chef prepared his famous roasted lamb for tonight."

"That is delicious." Jessica looked at Matt's eyes and took his hands between hers, trying to calm him down. "You're going to love it."

WHEN THEY HAD finished dinner, John invited the guests to move to the patio and enjoy coffee and liqueurs under the beautiful evening moonlight.

Jessica took advantage of a moment of privacy with Matt and asked, "Are we going to tell them?"

"It's not the right time," he muttered. "Didn't you see that your mother planned tonight's dinner to host the wonderful Tyler?" And then he mimicked Mary, "*You've been very successful in a famous New York firm, Tyler. Are you planning to continue your career there,*

Tyler? You should consider other factors besides a good job, Tyler. Your parents, and especially your mom, want you to marry Tyler and not me. Don't you see it?"

Jessica's eyes clouded. "I understand how you feel, and maybe they have other plans, but you need to keep in mind that I love you, and it doesn't matter what others think or do."

"I love you, too, Jess, but how can we be happy if they don't accept me?"

"That's not true. My parents are just worried about my future."

Matt was visibly nervous. "And that's why they've invited Tyler?"

"I don't know why my mom invited him; I don't care. As far as I know, it's just an old friend of the family."

"He wants to be more than that. Didn't you hear the comments about leaving his career in New York to come back here, and did you see how he looked at you?"

"That's his choice," Jessica began to sound distressed, "and it shouldn't impact us."

"I don't know, Jessica," he waved his hand, dismissing the comment. "I can't absorb all of this now. I'd better go."

"But why?" Her beautiful green eyes were wet with sorrow. "Can't you stay and just ignore them?"

"I don't want to argue with you. I'm sorry, but I'm leaving. If your parents ask, tell them I wasn't feeling well. I'll call you tomorrow."

Jessica's mother came to the living room. "The coffee is served." Her eyebrows raised. "What happened, Jessica? Why are you crying? Where is Matt?"

"Thanks for ruining this night, Mom," Jessica responded with a clenched jaw while making intense eye contact. "I was dreaming about this moment, and you've destroyed it. I hate you!" She ran upstairs to her room and locked the door.

"What's going on in here?" John said, entering the room. "What's the screaming about?"

Mary froze at the impact of her daughter's words. "I don't know. Jessica just went upstairs very distressed, and Matt left."

"It may be just a lover's fight. Don't worry. Just let her cool down. Tyler is on the patio, and we can't let him have coffee by himself."

The Daltons joined their guest, who had also heard some of the yelling.

"Everything okay?" Tyler smiled.

"I guess so. It was just a discussion between Jessica and Matt. He left, and she's upstairs. Sorry about that." Mary shook her head. "I don't think that relationship has much of a future. They are so different."

"What do you mean, Mary?"

"You know Jessica. She's bright, beautiful, went

to law school, and started her career as a lawyer, trying to be someone important in the future while he's a teacher." She had a grimace on her face. "What could he give her?"

"Mary, let's not bother our guest with our worries." John looked at Tyler. "Can I offer you a brandy or maybe some cognac?"

"Cognac would be the right thing for this beautiful evening." Tyler rubbed his hands together with a grin on his face.

The evening continued with light conversation mostly around Tyler's stories about how he had graduated with honors, was recruited by a top firm, and built a meteoric career in New York.

"But I think you mentioned coming back?" Mary leaned forward, looking into his eyes.

"Yes, it's something I've decided. I can't hide from you that I have feelings for Jessica and that it has been a major driving support in my decision, but she seems to be in a serious relationship."

Mary waved her hand, dismissing the comment. "Jessica's been in that relationship since she graduated, but you just saw tonight that they have some problems. I understand that you and Jessica did some dating while at school?"

"Yes, it started as flirting and lasted a few months, but then she graduated before I did and returned home while I decided to take a job opportunity. Anyway, now I miss this area, family, and friends."

"That's particularly important. Nothing can

replace being close to family and friends," Mary proclaimed with confidence.

"And you know the doors of the firm are always open for you," added John. "I know your father would be happy if you join us."

"I appreciate your candid comments, and I've already talked to my father about joining the firm. It has been a delightful evening, but I'm afraid I have to go now."

The Daltons stayed on the patio a little longer, enjoying the crisp night.

John looked at his wife. "What are you planning now?"

"Just thinking about our daughter's future."

"And I assume that it includes Tyler, right?"

"Don't you think that he would be a good choice?"

"Do you mean hers or *your* choice?"

"She's still young and maybe confused about what would be best for her. We, as parents, must help Jessica."

"And how are you going to do that?"

"I have some ideas. Now it's time to go to bed. I'll attend the board meeting at Lakeview tomorrow."

John rolled his eyes and shook his head. "I hope you know what you're doing."

Chapter 2

LAKEVIEW WAS ONE of the best private schools in the country, and the wealthiest families registered their children years in advance to secure admission. Making substantial financial contributions was also the right choice for those parents who wanted their children to graduate at the top of their class. A long list of Lakeview alumni in the country's top colleges built a successful business or political career.

That morning, as was scheduled every quarter, the principal, Mrs. Douglas, presented several topics related to the institution's status that usually included financial metrics, new projects, fundraising, and other general issues. The meetings were typically an opportunity for board members to ask questions, pretending to be smart in front of the others or have their names registered in the meeting records as proposing a motion of approval so everybody would know they had participated. The principal was skillful in handling those wealthy egos and successfully managing the meetings.

Eight out of the ten members were present when Mrs. Douglas opened the session. Everything went according to the normal routine until she got to the topics of general interest.

"Finally, I want to share two personnel decisions we have made recently," she paused and noticed the dull eyes of all members except for Mrs. Dalton, who seemed to show interest. "We've hired a new literature teacher to replace Mr. Brown, who announced his intention to retire, and we're promoting Mr. Hernandez to Head of the Department of Social Studies."

Mary raised her hand. "I know you have the authority to make those decisions, but could you share the background of those individuals?"

"Of course. I can make those decisions without board approval," the principal sighed, "but I'll be glad to share the information. The new literature teacher comes with valuable recommendations and eighteen years of experience in the field."

"And how about the promoted individual?" Mrs. Dalton asked impatiently.

"Mr. Hernandez has been with us for three years and demonstrated the kind of professional knowledge, leadership, and initiative that we believe will be a positive influence in our social studies department."

"Only three years? Is that enough experience to

run a department at this school? I'm not trying to step into your responsibilities but don't we have other options?"

"Mrs. Dalton, we agreed that this is not a board decision. I just brought this topic as a courtesy and for information purposes only as we normally do with general topics. I made the decision and take full responsibility for it." Then looking around, she said, "Any other questions before we close this session?"

Nobody wished to spend any more time on the topic and wanted to get out to carry on with their usual activities, except for Mary, who remained in the room and waited for everybody to leave.

"Excuse me, Mrs. Douglas. I didn't want to challenge your decision but was just trying to point out what I see as little experience to justify a promotion. It's your choice, and I respect it but thought that a different point of view could help you to make the right choice."

"I understand Mrs. Dalton and appreciate your contribution. We believe that it's the *right* choice. Now, if you will excuse me, I have to go back to my office."

"Please go and thank you for your report." Mary tried to hide her anger.

MARY DALTON WAS not a person to give up easily when she was after something and took the opportunity of having lunch to bring up the topic with her friends, Amy and Michelle.

"Do you know that at Lakeside, they are promoting a teacher with just three years of experience to become the head of a department?"

"Three years? Maybe he or she has some prior experience at other schools?" Amy asked while gobbling a chicken salad.

"No. The teacher is a young guy, and his only work experience has been at Lakeside."

Michelle laughed. "He must be a genius."

"Girls, this is serious. This promotion could impact the education of the children of our community, and you should think about it." Her jaw tightened.

"Sorry, we didn't mean to dismiss your comment," Amy apologized, "but do you think it's that serious?"

"I'm concerned and believe other parents should be, too. I heard this man is a social activist, and who knows what impact he's going to have if leading the social studies department."

"A social activist? Wow! We better share this with the people we know to see what can be done. I think my husband knows someone at the Private Schools Accreditation Commission. I'll ask him," replied Amy.

Michelle put her hand on her chin as if looking

for an answer and added, "Good idea. And my brother works at the state congress, so he may have some contacts also if needed."

"I knew you would help." Mary clapped her hands. "And we need to get more parents involved. How about if we bring the topic to the next PTA meeting? Michelle, as one of the PTA officers, could you include this topic on the agenda?"

"Wonderful idea." Her friend toasted with a glass of pinot grigio. "We will certainly do it."

The other two joined the celebration and continued talking about their usual round of gossip.

MEANWHILE, MATT RECEIVED a note from the school's principal asking him to stop by her office at the end of the school day. He anxiously went through the day's schedule, guessing that this had something to do with the promotion. Finally, the time came to visit the principal's office, and he knocked on the door.

"Please, come in," the familiar voice of Mrs. Douglas came through the door, "and have a seat so we can talk."

Matt nervously sat without saying a word, his hands quivering.

"You can relax, Mr. Hernandez. I have some good news for you." The principal smiled.

"Glad to hear that." Matt didn't know what else to say.

"We've talked before about the possibility of offering you the position of head of our social studies department," she paused to seize the effect of her words, "and now I would like to confirm that you're the new head of that department. Congratulations." She extended her hand.

"Thank you so much, Mrs. Douglas." He couldn't hide his excitement while shaking her hand. "I've been looking forward to this and promise that you'll be happy with the decision."

"We all hope so and wish you success with these new responsibilities." Mrs. Douglas slightly tilted her head and added, "Let me ask you something out of curiosity. Do you know people who might want to put obstacles in your career path?"

His jaw dropped and eyebrows raised. "You've taken me by surprise, but I can't think of anyone who would try to hurt my career. Why do you ask?"

She moved back in her chair, interlocked fingers under her chin. "Nothing especially, but I heard some comments challenging our decision to give the leadership position of the department to a young person with just a few years of experience."

"I hope it's not a problem for you or the school."

"Not at all. I've made the decision and fully support you, so go celebrate."

Matt left the principal's office smiling but with some concerns over who might be against his promotion? He called Jessica and asked her if she would be available for dinner.

"Of course, darling. I think we also need to talk about last night."

"Yes, Jessi. I'm sorry about what happened, but I have some good news I want to share. I'll see you at seven at the bistro near the waterfront market?"

"I'll be there. Counting the minutes." She blew him a kiss over the phone.

"See you later." Matt hung up and looked at his watch. He would be late for his meeting at the Protect Nature Alliance or PNA as it was usually called.

The meeting agenda included discussing the actions to be taken against the local brewery contaminating the river with dangerous water residues. It had been a long fight to promote legislation to force the implementation of purification processes and make sure the company complied with the regulations. For a couple of years, the PNA had organized community meetings and conferences to increase awareness about the public health risks associated with the operation of the facility owned by DB Corp., a nationally recognized brewery.

That evening about fifteen individuals gathered at the private room of a local restaurant owned by the association's president, Paul Peterson. The environment was tense because some drastic measures would have to be taken to answer the continuous lack of cooperation from DB Corp. The secretary read the meeting's agenda, and one of the attendees provided an update on the situation. A man in his forties with a firm tone of voice said, "The situation with the brewery has not changed. The latest report from the local authorities still shows non-compliance with existing regulations."

"That's not acceptable, and we need to do something immediately," shouted someone from the first row.

"Matt, please calm down, and let's wait to hear the full report," ordered the president with a stern look.

Matt didn't say anything but nodded in agreement. The report continued with the data sharing related to the level of contamination, a summary of the county's notifications to the company, and the association's previous actions. Regulations had officially been in effect for one year with a grace period of six months to allow the company to implement the appropriate process changes. DB Corp. applied for an extension of the grace period for an additional six months but had never managed to get any closer to compliance. Once the presentation ended, Matt requested permission to address the meeting.

"Paul," his voice dominated the room, "it is obvious that DB Corp. doesn't have any intention of complying with the regulations and is always trying to gain time supported by an army of lawyers. It wouldn't surprise me if we were in the presence of collaboration of local authorities that are easy in granting extensions."

"Matt," the president frowned, "you're making some serious accusations here. Do you have proof?"

"No, I don't, but nobody can deny that this delay in implementing a regulation that was supposed to be in effect a year ago should call for more drastic actions from the government. I would like to remind all of us that our friend, Brian Oliver, died just before he could share some important information he found in his investigation of DB Corp."

Most members nodded in approval and voiced their agreement with Matt as he continued.

"I propose we move to the second point in the agenda that is the definition of an action plan."

"Very well," Peterson mumbled. "I see that you're the presenter of that item, so please go ahead."

"Thank you, Paul." Matt moved to the front with firm steps. "I propose that we prepare a report with all the data we've collected during the last six months and request a meeting with the representatives of the company to discuss it."

"Why do we need to discuss with them something everybody knows?" someone asked.

"Because we eliminate the possibility of them saying we did not provide notice of our actions when we go to the authorities, demanding an answer to the lack of compliance." He paused to make sure everybody understood the strategy and continued, "Then we go to the authorities and tell them we're going to organize a protest in front of the facilities, demanding they make the required investments to treat the wastewater as needed."

"A protest?" The president's eyebrows arched. "Aren't we going too fast?"

"Paul, don't you think that it's time to do something? Otherwise, nobody will take our association seriously, and frankly, I don't know if I will continue being a member."

"Yes, let's do something," shouted a couple of people.

"People are getting sick, and fishing is being affected."

"We must take action," screamed another person.

The meeting developed into a chorus of complaints and insults against DB Corp. until the secretary called for order and the proposed action plan was approved.

JESSICA WAITED AT the bistro for fifteen minutes before Matt showed up and took a seat in front of her.

"Sorry, I'm late." He was agitated. "The meeting at the PNA took longer than expected, and I ran over here as soon as it ended."

She took his hand with a smile. "Don't worry. There's a nice view here, and I didn't mind waiting, so calm down." She stared into his eyes. "What happened? It looks like there's something else that worries you."

"You can see right through me, honey." He

composed himself. "But I don't want to spoil dinner with PNA problems."

"I know you need to share what is distressing you. I promise to listen. Please get it out, and then we can enjoy dinner."

"Okay. I still have the adrenaline flowing from the meeting. We heard a report confirming that the brewery has not yet implemented the changes needed to protect the water effluent, and we agreed to take some action. Those crooks have been playing around with the regulations and have done nothing to get into compliance."

"That's certainly disturbing." Her eyebrows raised. "How can they avoid compliance?"

"Because they have great lawyers," he paused, "and I also suspect good connections with the county agents."

"Do you mean bribes?" She tilted her head forward and put her hands onto the table. "But that's illegal."

"I can't prove it, but such a lack of interest from the authorities to implement the regulations seems suspicious."

"I can see why you're so upset."

He looked down. "There is something else…"

"What? You're beginning to worry me now." Her jaw tensed.

"I told you they have excellent lawyers."

His eyes continued to avoid hers.

"Oh, I see. I know DB Corp. is one of my dad's firm's clients, but what does it have to do with your concerns? Please tell me what you're thinking. Look at me," she demanded.

"DB Corp. has hired the services of Morris, Dalton, and Associates. Why would you think they need such a prestigious firm to defend them if they don't have something to hide?"

She was uneasy accepting her father could be defending a corporation that would play with the lives of many in the community and was a menace to the environment. "I'll talk to my father and see what he says."

"As you wish, but I think that it's good business for the firm. It's surely billing many hours to DB Corp."

"But my father always told me that ethics should have priority when accepting a case." She sounded disappointed.

"Okay, enough about this." He grinned. "I invited you for dinner to celebrate."

Her eyes were wide open. "Celebrate what?"

"You're in the presence of the new head of the social studies department at Lakeview."

"Wow, congratulations," she exclaimed and rose to hug him. "I knew you were going to get it."

"Mrs. Douglas told me this afternoon."

"And it's been endorsed by the board?"

"Yes, everything has been approved."

She took a big bite of her shrimp salad. "That's so exciting."

"The only thing that puzzled me was a comment from the principal."

"What did she say? And by the way, this salad is delicious."

"She asked whether I knew someone who would want to put obstacles in my career path."

"Who could it be? You don't have any enemies because you're so adorable." Her eyes were beaming.

"She said people were challenging her decision, and I've been thinking…."

"What's bothering you?"

"I know she had to share her decision with the board, and I know your mom is a member."

"Are you serious?" Her eyebrows drew in, and her lips narrowed. "Are you insinuating that my mom wants to hurt your career?"

"Calm down. I'm just saying the only person I know who has shown some disdain toward me is your mom, and I can't figure out whether she would try to influence Mrs. Douglas's decision."

"Matt, not again. Yesterday you left our house because you assumed my parents invited Tyler to get him closer to me, and now *this*. I don't know if I can live with this continuous fight." She began weeping.

"Please, don't cry. But you have to agree that it's very suspicious."

"Why can we have a moment without talking

about your sick feelings related to a conspiracy from my parents. Maybe you need to gain their respect and love instead of complaining all the time." She picked up her purse and left.

Chapter 3

THE DALTON'S WERE having dinner at home when they heard the front door open, followed by quick steps toward the stairs leading to the bedrooms. Jessica seemed upset, and Mary got up and put her arms around her daughter.

"What's going on, Jessica? Please, come join us. We thought you were having dinner with Matt and didn't wait for you. Did you eat anything?"

"Just an appetizer." Sobs shook her body. "It's been a terrible evening."

"Okay, calm down. Have something to eat, and you'll see that you'll feel better."

"I'm not hungry," protested Jessica.

"Honey, we know you're suffering from something, but starving yourself will not solve anything. Do what your mother is suggesting and share your concerns. We're here with you," said John, putting his hand on Jessica's shoulder and offering her a glass of water.

She sat down, still sobbing but feeling more comfortable. "I think you were right."

"Right about what, dear?" Mary opened her eyes, and her eyebrows raised.

"About Matt," Jessica lowered her voice.

Mary looked at her husband with a triumphant smile.

John looked at her, leaning forward. "What happened with him?"

"It's just that he always thinks that everybody is against him."

"Why? Who could do something to him? Does he have enemies?"

"No, he's well-liked, but sometimes he imagines things. For example, we were supposed to celebrate his promotion, but he's worried about some comments someone made to the principal, challenging his qualifications for the position."

John stared at his wife.

"Oh, I'm sure someone was expecting to be selected and may be jealous and could have made some comments," Mary said quickly.

"I don't know, Mom, but it looks like he can't just enjoy life and is always worried about something."

"There are people like that, and it's difficult for them to change," emphasized Mary.

"Let's not make a big deal out of this. Have something to eat, and after getting some sleep, you'll see things differently tomorrow," John interrupted with a scornful look from his wife.

"Maybe you're right. Thanks, Dad." A bite of the delicious lasagna made her feel better already.

They finished dinner, and Jessica got up to go to her room. "Thanks, Mom and Dad. I know I can count on you. Goodnight."

"Goodnight, dear," Mary responded with a smile, but as soon as her daughter left, she turned to her husband.

He glared at his wife with a clenched jaw, furrowed brows, and a reddish face. "What have you done? She's beginning to feel disappointed at *that* boyfriend, and you have to say, *let's not make a big deal*?"

"And what were you trying to do by making comments about his qualifications for the promotion? Don't tell me you didn't do it because I know you mentioned yesterday that you were going to the Lakeview board meeting."

"I'm just trying to protect our daughter from making a big mistake."

"Are you protecting her by trying to take what she loves out of her life?"

"She's too young and doesn't know what is best for her."

"Do you?" John began walking out of the room. "I hope you don't do something you'll regret later."

She ignored his comment while thinking about her next move.

ON THE FOLLOWING day, John was in a meeting with his partner, Frank Morris, Tyler, Jessica, and some other associates. Frank was proudly announcing that his son had decided to join the firm when an assistant came into the room.

"Sorry to interrupt, Mr. Morris, but you have an urgent phone call."

Frank stared at her. "And who's calling that can't wait?"

"It's Mr. Brackman, and he insisted on interrupting you."

"You better take the call, Frank," said John. "DB Corp. is our best customer, and we can't let their president wait if there is something urgent to attend to."

Frank got up. "You're right. I better take this." He went to his office, sat on his high black leather chair, and swiveled to look at the nice downtown view from his window while picking up the phone. "Hello, Don, what can I do for you?"

"Hi, Frank. Sorry to take you out of your meeting, but there is a new development that may require some action on your part."

"I'm listening. From your tone, it sounds like you're worried about something."

"Yes, I am. You know we've been delaying the implementation of the wastewater treatment project for financial reasons."

"Yes, and we've made the presentation, claiming force majeure to the authorities."

"The authorities are not the problem but rather the environmentalists. The PNA developed an action plan that includes protests and contacts with the press."

"I thought Peterson had the PNA under control for you."

"He's still on our side, but at yesterday's meeting, things got out of hand. A couple of individuals began a claim for action and the rest followed."

"I see. It looks like we need to warn the authorities that the PNA will probably present a petition to organize a demonstration, and we need to block it. We have some contacts in the media that can be alerted to focus on the potential for violence that the PNA actions may create."

"Thanks, Frank. I knew you were going to protect us as usual."

"One more question. Did Peterson mention the names of the leaders pushing for the protest against DB Corp.? We may investigate them to see if we can find something to take them out of it."

"He did mention a young guy named Matt

Hernandez as the apparent leader of the radicalized group."

"Okay. Thank you. We'll start working on this immediately." Frank went back to the meeting room and shared the content of his conversation with Brackman.

When John heard the name of the individual leading the complaints, he exhaled, crossing his arms. *Jessica, I think your mother is right*, he thought.

IN THE MEANTIME, Matt called the PNA task force members to develop and implement the action plan against DB Corp. agreed upon the day before. It was a small group, but they were convinced of what they should do. They asked for a meeting with the company's president, but given the request's short notice, Mrs. Williams, the Public Relations Manager, agreed to receive them that afternoon.

Matt told his team, "If the president doesn't want to see us, let's go anyway because we know they will give all sorts of excuses. We want to put them on notice that the community will not accept any more delays to address compliance with wastewater regulations."

At four o'clock that afternoon, Matt and two other PNA members introduced themselves to the DB Corp. receptionist, who called the PR manager's office. A few minutes later, a young woman with a friendly smile showed up.

"Mr. Hernandez?"

Matt moved forward. "That's me, and these are my associates from Protect Nature Alliance."

She maintained her smile. "I'm Mrs. Williams's assistant. She's waiting for you in our board room. Let me take you there, please."

Board room? They are trying to impress us, thought Matt.

They got to the second floor and entered the room where a woman in her forties was reading some documents. As soon as she saw them, she got up to greet them.

"Hi, I'm Laura Williams. Nice to meet you all. Mr. Brackman sends his apologies for not being here, but he had to go out of town on an urgent trip and asked me to receive you."

They sat down in burgundy leather chairs at one end of the magnificent table, went through the usual introductions, and the assistant offered them all coffee or water, which the visitors politely refused. Once she left, Matt looked around the room, noticing the expensive furniture, the top-of-the-line communications equipment, and a couple of beautiful works of art.

"It looks like business is going quite well from what I can see."

Laura looked at him with a forced smile. "Mr.

Hernandez, this is a large corporation, and the board expects to have a meeting place according to the importance of the company. In this room, the executives host important guests, and it is also offered to auditors to conduct their reviews and gather the information they need. We try to provide a comfortable set-up for those external visitors." She paused. "Let's move to the purpose of this urgent request."

"Thank you, Mrs. Williams." Matt leaned on the table with an intent gaze. "As you should know, DB Corp. has not been complying with wastewater regulations despite receiving an additional six-month grace period that has passed. The PNA considers this an unacceptable behavior for a thriving corporation and is ready to take action unless there is an improvement in the water effluents coming from the facilities owned by DB Corp."

Laura also leaned on the table. "I hope that's not a threat." Then she regained her calm posture, maintaining eye contact. "It's understandable that the PNA has some concerns since this has been a long process. You correctly mentioned that the county authorities granted a grace period given the company's difficulties in implementing the required equipment changes. This project requires a substantial investment and importing parts with a long delivery time. DB Corp. introduced a request for an extension of the grace period, claiming force majeure because a major supplier of equipment based in Italy declared bankruptcy. The approval of the extension period is still pending but has not been denied, so DB Corp. is not out of compliance."

Matt raised his eyebrow and widened his eyes. "The regulations were approved more than a year ago. Are you telling us that the company is not out of compliance?"

"That is correct. We have not been able to implement the project for different circumstances that the authorities are aware of," the manager replied with a firm voice.

"Mrs. Williams, I'm afraid that we have a different view on this issue, and we wanted to alert the company about our position and the possibility that we'll start a campaign to make the community aware of the situation."

"Mr. Hernandez, I guess we can agree to disagree, and we'll be happy to explain where the project is as I have done with you today. Unless there is something else I can do for you, it seems that this meeting is over."

As soon as the visitors left, Laura went to the office next door. The man sitting behind a sizeable wood-carved desk raised his eyes. "Have they gone now?"

"Yes, Mr. Brackman. We just finished the meeting."

"And what do they want?"

"They came to tell us that our delay in imple-menting the wastewater project is unacceptable, and they are ready to take action if we don't comply with the regulations."

He rose from the seat and banged his fist over the desk, shouting, "And who they think they are to tell me how to run my business. Who were those individuals?"

"There were three of them, but only one spoke. Matt Hernandez."

Brackman sat, exhaling while turning his head toward a window and clenching his hands. "I've heard that name already." He looked back at Laura. "Tell Joe Brown, the head of security, to come to my office now."

He picked up the phone as soon as she left. "Peterson, you're becoming useless."

A brief silence followed on the other side of the line. "What happened now, Mr. Brackman?" replied the PNA head, pretending to be calm.

"Your boys just came to my office, threatening us."

"I told you some people were becoming excited around here."

Brackman lost his temper and shouted, "You need to keep everything under control and not just tell me how things are going there. If you can't handle it, maybe the association should elect a new president." He hung up and waved in the head of security.

Joe Brown was an ex-cop in his fifties with broad

shoulders and an athletic complexion who had worked with Brackman for ten years. He would do whatever his boss ordered without asking and with no fear of consequences because he knew the boss would protect him.

"What can I do for you, Mr. Brackman?"

"You need to investigate a man named Matt Hernandez. He's with the PNA and meddling too much in our business. I need to know everything you can find on him—work, relations, family—you name it. We must find his weak spot."

"Okay, Mr. Brackman."

"And we need it right now, so leave everything else and focus on this guy."

"Will do." And he left the office.

We'll see how far we need to go to silence you, thought Brackman while lighting a cigar.

At the same time, Peterson scheduled an urgent meeting of the PNA for the next day at his restaurant. The agenda had only two points: a report from the meeting with DB Corp. officials and a review of the action plan.

Chapter 4

MICHELLE WAS PREPARING breakfast when the phone rang. "Why are you calling this early, my friend. Is anything wrong?"

"No, Michelle," the excited voice of Mary Dalton replied, "I just wanted to catch you before you go about your day. I have some good news."

"What is it, girl? You intrigue me."

"Jessica was distraught last night."

"And seeing your daughter upset makes you happy?" There was sarcasm in Michelle's voice.

"Of course not. What makes me happy is the cause of her being upset."

"Let me guess. Something to do with the boyfriend?"

"*Yes.* Matt invited Jessica to a surprise dinner to share the news of his promotion, and somehow they got into a big argument. She left the restaurant and came home, crying."

"Is it over then?"

"Not sure, but just in case, we need to continue with our plan. Have you included the topic of the promotion on the agenda?"

"Not only that, but I convinced the PTA to advance the meeting for this Friday after they received the required two-day notice."

"Wonderful. You're an angel. Let me ask you another question."

"One more Machiavellian idea?"

Mary chuckled. "Kind of. Isn't your daughter attending Matt's class?"

"Yes." Michelle was puzzled.

"And what does she think about him?"

"She hates him. He's very demanding, and my daughter says that behind his friendly approach, he's ruthless."

"That's what other parents told me also. Do you think your daughter would help us get rid of Matt?"

"I'm sure she would love that, but what could she do?"

"Let me tell you a plan B in case we don't get support from the PTA." The two ladies continued with their conversation.

THE MEETING OF the PNA started at four that afternoon. Matt was responsible for reporting back from their meeting at DB Corp. offices. He stood up and raised his voice. "As we suspected, the official at DB Corp. didn't provide any satisfactory answers. The president refused to see us, and their PR manager just gave us a story indicating that they are not out of compliance."

Some members raised voices of disapproval, and Peterson called for order. "Let's be more specific and try to understand what they are saying. Matt, can you provide more details explaining their position? Why does DB Corp. claim to comply with the regulations?"

"They say the company requested another extension for implementation of the project, claiming force majeure for a delay in receiving imported equipment."

"And do we know whether it's true?"

"DB Corp. bought the equipment from an Italian company they claim declared bankruptcy."

"Is that the case? Because if it is, they may have a valid justification."

"We cannot validate that."

"And what are the authorities saying regarding the requested extension?"

"The company did not receive an answer yet," Matt began to get frustrated because he saw where this was going.

"So, if the company is claiming that the equipment for the project has not arrived and the authorities have not responded yet, wouldn't it be possible that the delay in the response may be related to the investigation on whether the story of the Italian company going bankrupt is true?"

"Maybe," Matt muttered.

Peterson seized the moment. "I think we need to be careful with our reactions. While we have the perception that they are refusing to comply, there could be elements that justify their behavior. Let's move to the discussion of the action plan."

Matt spoke again. "We concluded that DB Corp. is just coming up with excuses to avoid implementing the water-treatment project, and therefore, our association has the responsibility to take visible action."

"And what would that be?"

"As a first step, we propose to organize a march in front of the brewery. We'll call the media to cover the event so the public is aware of the situation and force the authorities to intervene. The second phase would be to continue the awareness campaign at the national level. The third step would be to initiate legal actions against the company and its officers as needed."

"I believe that plan is too aggressive," Peterson was agitated. "How can we start a protest when it's not clear whether the company is creating excuses, as you said, or truly impacted by a delay in receiving the equipment? Don't you think it would be irresponsible for us to steer the public against DB Corp. without having an accurate knowledge of the situation? We could put our association in danger of being sued and discredited. I think we need to reassess the circumstances and revise the proposed action plan."

"Paul, we have been evaluating this situation for months and never made progress in improving the quality of the water as the regulations mandate. It's time to act, and the time is *now*." A solid fist-shaking accompanied Matt's loud voice and determination.

"Matt, we need to calm down and not let passion lead our actions. We need facts. While we're all frustrated, we must remain cool to evaluate what we'll do next. I propose we do not accept the action plan as presented and reassess it after gathering some data on the Italian supplier's bankruptcy. I assume the authorities are working on it, and we can consult with them." He looked around for reactions and continued, "At this point, I would like to call for a vote on the proposed action plan versus the alternative I just mentioned. All in favor of reassessing the action plan, please raise your hands."

Six hands went up out of the twelve members present. "I see that there is a tie, and our bylaws indicate that the president has the decisive vote. My vote, therefore, is to amend the proposed action plan and ask the secretary of the association to register our decision."

As soon as everybody left, Peterson got on the phone. "Good afternoon, Mr. Brackman."

"I hope you have some good news for me," a demanding voice replied.

"Our team members reported back from the meeting they had yesterday with your PR manager."

"And?" the voice grew impatient.

"They didn't believe the story of the force majeure and proposed an action plan that included a march in front of the plant."

"*What*?" Now Brackman was furious.

"Don't worry. I took care of it, and the action plan was not approved, for now."

"What do you mean *for now*? Can't you make it disappear?"

"It's not that easy. Everybody is upset, and I barely got the plan for a protest rejected by casting my vote to untie the vote count."

"Is that Hernandez guy making all the noise again?"

"He's the leader of the group that wants to go to the streets. Hernandez was at your office yesterday."

"I know that. I think you need to do something to discredit Hernandez before he can do too much damage."

"I'll try, but as I said, there are other association members who align with him."

"Do something with him, then, to break the alignment. I'm sure you'll find a way." And the phone went dead.

Brackman called his assistant. "Tell Mr. Kowalski, the head of the local union, to come to my house this evening."

The relations between the local union and the company had been stable for some time. Don Brackman had built trust by giving the union leaders certain perks and recognition, as he liked to call discrete monetary contributions. It was not unusual to see the union leaders and their families enjoying a barbeque at the residence of the DB Corp. president.

MATT AND HIS friends, Josh and Mike, who aligned with him in the PNA discussion, went to a bar close to the location where the meeting had just finished.

"I can't believe what Peterson is doing." Matt was furious.

"It seems that he trusts too much what DB Corp. is saying." Josh nodded with an uneven smile.

Matt read his friend's body expression. "Do you think that he's working with them?"

"That can't be true," added Mike, raising his eyebrows.

"Didn't you see how agitated he became when Matt presented the action plan?"

"And how he accused me of being too passionate about this," Matt reminded them.

"But he's been the president of PNA for many years," tried to reason Mike, "and we've seen him involved in several cases against big corporations. It's hard to believe that he would have any hidden motivation to delay action now."

"Don't know whether he has, but we need to do something," Matt continued. "The PNA may decide to wait, but nothing prevents us from contacting the media to tell the story."

"Peterson wouldn't approve it," mumbled Mike.

"He can influence and decide what the association will do, but he can't prevent a worried citizen from sharing his concerns." Matt gazed at his friend.

Josh put his right elbow on the table, holding his chin with his hand. "I know someone who works at Channel 5. Maybe she can help us."

Matt smiled for the first time in the day. "That would be great."

"Okay. I'll call my contact and see whether she would meet us and is interested in the story."

"Another thing. I believe we need to take a sample of the wastewater from the brewery."

"But they won't allow us to get in their site."

"We can get a sample in the river just downstream from the brewery. It's not exactly the point where the inspectors check it for compliance, but it could give us a data point to have an idea of how bad the problem is."

Mike looked down. "And when do you want to do that?"

"How about tonight? I don't see any reason to wait, and if Josh's friend agrees to talk to us, we'll have something to show her."

Josh was ready to follow his friend. "Okay. I'm in."

"If you'll excuse me, I'm afraid I won't be able to go. I already have something planned for tonight."

"Don't worry, Mike. Josh and I can take care of this, and we'll keep you posted."

"Please do," Mike said while getting up and leaving.

MATT WAS DRIVING his Toyota. "Do you think Mike is not too convinced about what we're doing?"

"I don't know. Maybe he's just concerned about what Peterson may say."

"Yes, but I don't think we should worry about Mike. He's just too cautious. Look, the lab is on the right."

Matt parked in front of the lab the PNA had used in the past. When they went inside, a technician received them with a smile.

"Hello. It has been quite some time without seeing you around here. How can I help you?"

Matt gave him a firm handshake. "Hi, Oscar. We need to get some test tubes and the protocol to test the brewery wastewater."

"That's not so simple, gentlemen. May I ask what you are trying to do?"

"We want to take a sample in the river downstream from the brewery because we believe their wastewater is causing all sorts of problems with fish and marine life. Once we get the sample, we'll bring it to you to run the analysis."

"I'll be happy to help but be aware that compliance is verified by the state taking a thirty-day average and a seven-day average per sample, so a spot sample will not prove anything."

"Okay. I understand, but we would like to try one sample to get some indication, and if it's as bad as we think, then we can go with the formal process."

"Do you have permission from the brewery to take the sample at the discharge point of the waste-water? That's where it should be taken."

"No, I don't think they would give as the authorization," insisted Matt, getting a little impatient. "Are you going to help us or not?"

"Yes, of course. I just wanted to let you know that what you're doing is not going to prove anything."

"We know, but as I said, we're trying to at least

get something that can help us to get more support for this case."

"Perfect. I understand." Oscar left for a moment and came back with a couple of test tubes and a copy of the state's regulations regarding wastewater treatment. "It's a long read, but I suggest looking at chapter ten on how to collect samples."

"Thanks, Oscar. We'll see you tomorrow." The two friends left and got into Matt's car.

Josh was getting excited about this adventure. "Now we need to get by my father's house to borrow his boat."

"Why do we need a boat?"

"Because we'll need to take a sample a few feet from the shore. Otherwise, it could get contaminated with sediment."

"Glad you're with me."

"You're always into the action but need someone to help you think." Josh smiled.

They stopped by Josh's parents' and left one hour before sunset. The brewery was about fifty miles north of town, and Matt drove the last few miles on a dirt road that took them to the river not too far from the plant's boundaries. The small boat trailer's sound going over the road's bumps provided the only break to the tense silence.

With the last light of the day, they arrived at the river and rapidly deployed the boat. A metal barrier thirty feet away indicated the limit of the brewery's site. Josh got into the boat first, and Matt followed, taking the oars. A few minutes passed until they positioned themselves to take the samples. Josh carefully submerged the tubes, collected the water, and put them in a protective case.

"Done," shouted Josh with a triumphant smile.

Matt's eyes were bright with enthusiasm. "Good job, partner."

They got back to shore, put the boat back onto the trailer, and were ready to go home.

"What are you doing?" a voice shouted from behind the fence.

"Nothing that should matter to you. We're on public land," Matt's attitude was defiant.

"Saw you taking water samples. It seems unusual at this time of the day. I was simply curious." He had a much more amicable tone.

"Since you're asking more politely, I'll explain." Matt was gaining time while thinking about what to say. "We're running an experiment with our students at Lakeview School and collected some water to identify different forms of marine life through lab analysis. By the way, can you tell us approximately the distance from here to the brewery's wastewater discharge?"

"It's about three hundred yards from this point."

"Perfect. I just wanted to make sure we weren't too close. The distance is okay and will not impact the results. Thank you and have a good evening."

They got back onto the dirt road. "Do you think the guard suspected anything?" Josh's voice was tense.

"No, he's just a guard making his round, but just in case, I told him the story about the school experiment."

It was already dark when they returned the boat to Josh's parents.

His mother had a broad smile. "We thought that by now you must be hungry, so why don't you stay and have dinner with us?"

"She made your favorite chicken with plum sauce." Josh's father beamed.

Matt had known Josh's parents for many years and couldn't refuse. He enjoyed the childhood stories about Josh's father wondering how the rabbits would manage to get into his garden and eat the carrots. Now he understood that the good man was pretending to be puzzled while enjoying the faces of Josh and his friends, barely containing their laugh.

Dinner was exquisite, and the conversation was animated. At some point, Josh shared what they were doing.

"Something is going on with that plant. A bunch of fishermen I know keep complaining about how fish are not as abundant as they used to be and are even found floating dead sometimes."

"Oxygen depletion from a large volume of contaminants in the water could cause it." Matt shared what he had learned through many hours of investigation on the impact that poorly treated wastewater could cause in rivers and the sea.

Josh's father leaned forward. "And why isn't something being done?"

"There are regulations that address the issue, but the problem is lack of compliance," his son exhaled while crossing his arms, "and that's why we're taking samples to see if we can get some data and mobilize people to demand corrective actions."

"That's good." Josh's father was getting excited. "If you need help, I can put you in contact with my fishermen friends so you can explain it to them."

"That would be wonderful," Matt shared the enthusiasm. "Just let us know when we can talk to them and explain why they're catching fewer fish."

"I'm pretty sure they will be interested and help you as needed."

They continued talking about the damage that progress had been inflicting to nature and how action would be needed to contain if not reverse the problem. Then the two friends left, and Matt took Josh to his apartment before going home after such a busy day.

Chapter 5

WHEN JOHN DALTON went to his office early in the morning, his partner, Frank, wanted to meet and share some news from a phone call with their main client, Don Brackman, the previous night.

"John, we need to get together. Brackman called me last night, and he's not happy with the attention the PNA is giving to their operation."

"Okay, Frank. Let me finish something I have on my hands. Should we meet in thirty minutes? How about if we ask Tyler and Jessica to join, so they start getting an understanding of the DB Corp. account?"

"Fine with me. I think it is going to be good that they hear it."

At nine, the two partners and their children got together in the elegant meeting room with a magnificent river view, and Frank began.

"I got a call last night from Mr. Brackman,

sharing his concerns on what he sees as unsolicited investigations of their operation."

"Does he want to start legal action against someone?" John tapped his pen in a notebook.

"Not yet, but he is asking for our advice on how to handle the case. It is a legal as well as a public relations issue." Frank turned to Jessica. "This could be an interesting project for you."

Jessica's eyes brightened. "A project with the number one customer of the firm? That would be awesome."

"Yes, a great opportunity, but hold your enthusiasm until you know all the details." Frank raised his hand slowly.

"Okay, can we go to the point?" Tyler gazed at his father. *Why would she get that assignment and not me?*

"Remember that a couple of days ago, Brackman called to express his concerns about the PNA being active in planning some action against his company?"

"Yes, and you told him that we might have some contacts in the media to fence off any bad publicity against him." John opened his arms while leaning on his chair.

"Correct. Well, things are moving at a faster speed than we thought. A small group of PNA representatives went to DB Corp. offices and threatened their PR manager about taking some immediate action if the company does not comply with waste-water regulations."

"But we have presented a petition in their name asking for an extension of time for the implementation of the project based on delays in the delivery of imported equipment," John argued, like being in front of a judge. "Didn't the PR manager explain it to the PNA people?"

"Yes, she did, but they wouldn't listen, saying that it is just a delay tactic to avoid implementing the project."

Tyler waved his hand. "That's their problem."

"There's more," Frank looked around at all of them, "last night a couple of PNA guys went by the river, next to the brewery fence line, and took some water samples."

"It looks like they're serious." Jessica's hands steepled.

"Doesn't Brackman have a good relationship with the president of the PNA?" John asked.

"He does, but there's a group within the PNA that's not responding to the president. Fortunately, he has good sources of information and is aware of everything the small group is doing. He thinks it's mainly a couple of individuals who are leading this escalade against DB Corp. They were the visitors to DB Corp. offices and the same who went last night to take the water samples from the river."

"Wow, pretty belligerent guys." Tyler's eyebrows arched. "Do we know who they are to see if we can find something against them?"

"Yes, we heard the same name again." Frank

looked down at the desk. "Matt Hernandez is the leader." He raised his head and met Jessica's eyes. "You know him well. Do you think you can talk to him and find out what he is up to?"

"I could try. We're not on the best terms right now, but I can certainly talk to Matt and see if he can understand the company's position."

"That would be good." Her father felt proud. "And if he wants to talk to us and discuss the status of the corporation's petition for an extended time for compliance, we would be happy to receive him in the office."

"Okay, Jessica," Frank nodded, "it looks like you're on a mission, representing our firm. Good luck."

The meeting ended, and Tyler was a little jealous about Jessica getting the action, but on the other hand, happy to know that Matt Hernandez could be in trouble. He followed Jessica to her office, closed the door behind him, sat across from her desk, slightly lowered his head, and smiled with a probing look.

"Did you know that your boyfriend was so active in protecting the environment?"

"I know he is interested in social causes, including environmental protection, but I'm a little surprised to learn about the things he allegedly did."

"C'mon Jessica, don't let love affect your intellect. What we heard would show that he is sort of obsessed with this and thinks he can save the world."

"I wouldn't judge right now and prefer to hear what he has to say." She reclined in her chair.

"If I were you, I would tell him he is getting into major trouble if he continues with that behavior." Tyler raised his voice and leaned toward the desk.

"Thanks for the advice," Jessica regained her posture, "but I think I know how to handle this situation. I have known Matt for a few years and believe he may have good reasons to do what he is doing. I will listen and reason with him." Her tone was not reassuring.

"Okay. Good luck, and you know that I'll always be here for you."

As soon as Tyler left, Jessica called Matt.

"Hi. How are you doing today?"

"Hi." Matt was not too sure how to handle this, considering her abrupt departure the last time they were together. "Doing great. You got me during my lunch break."

"I knew you would answer at this time and would like to see you today if you can." Her tone was sweet and warm.

"Of course. I thought you were mad at me after our last encounter."

"I have to admit I was upset, but I believe we need to talk. How about dinner at the bistro? Let's see if we can finish that delicious meal this time," she giggled. "My treat."

"Okay. I'll be there at seven. Looking forward to having a peaceful conversation. I missed you."

"Me too. See you then."

MATT HAD A good feeling after a few days of tension. Josh had delivered the samples to the lab that morning, he'd had an uneventful day with the students, and now Jessica wanted to see him. However, his happiness didn't last long because he bumped into Mrs. Williams in the hallway when returning to his class.

"Hello, Matt. It looks like someone is still trying to hurt you."

"What do you mean, Mrs. Williams?" Matt frowned.

"Just received the agenda for the PTA meeting. There is a topic about the new head of social studies selection, and they asked me to attend."

"Do you know why?"

"No, but don't worry. No matter what they may say, *you* are the head of the department."

"Thank you, Mrs. Williams. I would like to know what the parents have to say if you can share it with me."

"I'll let you know."

She left, but Matt's humor changed again. *What*

could be the concern now? Who would be behind this? His mind was looking for answers.

THE BISTRO BY the waterfront market was packed. Laughter and loud voices indicated that alcohol was flowing freely and people were having a good time. Jessica had made a reservation for a quiet table on the terrace, and they were seated in a corner that barely resembled calmness.

It's okay; we need to get some cheering, too, she thought as the hostess showed her to the table where Matt was waiting and stood up as soon as she got closer. She kissed him on the cheek.

"Hi, honey. How was your day?"

"Not too exciting until now. Just the school and dealing with the students. Today they were okay, but sometimes you wonder why they go to school if they don't show any interest."

She smiled. "Don't you remember when we were in high school? The latest gossip about others and especially the faculty was far more important than whatever the teacher was saying."

"You're right. I can't complain much now when we went through the same," he said, holding Jessica's hand. "How have you been? The last time we got together, we had an unfortunate ending. Are you still mad at me?"

"I told you on the phone that it was a reaction in the moment, and I'm here so you can see I still love you." She squeezed his hand.

"Good. Let's forget about that night and order something delicious. I have to warn you that I'm starving." His eyes worked through the menu.

"A good appetite is a sign of good health, so go ahead. I told you it's my treat today." Jessica opened the menu, but her eyes looked at Matt while licking her lips. "Do you want to order for me, too? You know what I like."

"I think you're trying to distract me from choosing my dish, but I'll be happy to order for both of us. I think we're both in the mood for oysters." Matt grinned.

"Wow. You're reading my mind. I told you that you know me."

They had a good time, enjoying the food and remembering past stories.

He looked into her eyes. "We've certainly had good moments. I wish everything would continue to be that way."

"And why wouldn't it? Anything worrying you?"

"I would say that sometimes things get more complicated than we would like them to."

"But you just got a promotion. Aren't you happy?"

"Yes, but Mrs. Williams told me this afternoon

that the PTA has requested her presence at their next meeting to talk about my qualifications."

"The PTA doesn't have any authority over her decisions related to the staff. Is she afraid of the PTA?"

"No. She told me not to worry, but I can't stop wondering who may be behind it." Matt's eyes still evaded hers.

Jessica exhaled, and her shoulder hunched. "I know what you think."

"Jessica, please, I don't want to fight again over it," he interrupted.

"Let me finish," her eyes clouded, "I know that you believe my mother may have something to do, but I'm behind you, so no matter who may be involved, I believe that you deserve the promotion. Just let time pass, and everything will be okay." Her reassuring smile felt like a breath of fresh air to him.

"Thank you, Jessica. I love you."

"How about we go skiing this weekend to relax a little?"

"That's a good idea. I'm busy with some activities with the PNA, but I think I can work in time for skiing around it."

"I haven't seen you so engaged with a PNA issue before. I heard that you were taking some water samples by the river last night."

Matt's eyes opened, and he sat up straight, leaning his body forward. "How do you know I was taking samples?" The tone of his voice surprised Jessica.

"What's the matter?" Jessica looked confused. "We were at a meeting this morning with my father, his partner, and Tyler, reviewing the DB Corp. account when my father's partner mentioned that Don Brackman called him, worried about the PNA activities against his company."

"And how did my name get brought up in the conversation?"

"Brackman indicated that you visited their offices, making some threats, and then went to the river, near the brewery."

"I can't believe it," said Matt with an intense brightness in his eyes and a clenched jaw.

Jessica still didn't understand all the excitement. "Why are you mad? Was it a secret?"

"No, but we decided to go for that sample yesterday right after the PNA meeting, so how would Brackman know I was involved?"

"Maybe someone knows you were by the river?"

"I went to the river with Josh, and nobody was around. It was also getting dark. A sentinel at the brewery saw us, but he doesn't know my name, so it has to be someone else." Matt's brain was revisiting every hour of the previous day.

"And who knew you were going to take the sample? Maybe someone at the PNA?"

"We suspect that Peterson, the PNA president,

is working closely with Brackman, so he could have told him. But Peterson didn't know our plan because we discussed it after the meeting."

"And who did you discuss the plan with?"

"Eureka," Matt snapped his fingers, "you're a genius," and before Jessica could say a word, "it was *Mike,* that traitor." His fist banged the table.

"Calm down; people are looking."

Matt was fighting to control his anger. "You're right. Sorry."

"Do you want to tell me what it is?"

"Yesterday, after the PNA meeting, I went to a bar with Josh and Mike to discuss what to do given Peterson's negative to take action against DB Corp. We were throwing out ideas, and I proposed taking a water sample to get an idea of the river contamination. Josh asked when and I said why not now. He immediately offered to join, but Mike put out an excuse not to come with us."

"So, you think that Mike not only didn't go but alerted Peterson on what you were going to do?"

"It's the only explanation. Brackman couldn't have known so soon unless Peterson told him, and in turn, Peterson couldn't have known unless Mike told him. That *traitor.*"

"Wow. It looks like an espionage movie with all those alliances and spies."

"Unfortunately, it is."

"And why is this so important?"

"Because we believe the brewery is presenting excuses to avoid investing in reducing wastewater residues and complying with the regulations. In the meantime, water pollution has reduced marine life, and fishermen are losing their source of income."

"I heard the delay in completing the project is due to lack of imported equipment and a petition for additional time has been presented but not resolved yet."

Matt shook his head. "I'm convinced that those are excuses. You hear the stories that Brackman tells your father, and I don't blame him for protecting his client, but why so many coincidences? An equipment manufacturer goes bankrupt, an unresolved petition for additional time, a close relationship between DB Corp. and the PNA president. Now, what looks like the PNA president having spies among my friends, it's too much, and I'm not going to stop."

"It certainly looks like there are a lot of unanswered questions, but I'm concerned that your passion for this cause could lead you down a dangerous path," Jessica mumbled, looking at her glass. "Do you think that would help if you went to our office and talked to my father and his partner? I don't know, but maybe if they learn about the water contamination and the impact on the fishermen's jobs, they could do something."

"Jessica, I appreciate your concerns, but DB Corp. is their client, and I assume they have to defend their position. You know now why I'm so involved in this, and if you want to share what I told you, feel free to try. If Morris, Dalton, and Associates want to get data on the levels of contamination and environmental impact of the brewery's operation, I would be happy to visit and talk about it." He looked at her. "Let's leave this topic now. You've helped me a lot, and I would like to end the evening on a happy note."

"But my father…"

He put his finger on her lips softly. "Stop, Jessica. We should not discuss what your parents are doing or not doing. I believe in you and love you, and everything else is not important."

"That's right. I love you, too." Her lips brushed his hand with a kiss.

Chapter 6

ANTONI KOWALSKI ARRIVED at the Brackman's mansion in the evening. He parked the truck in the big circular driveway, wondering why Brackman had required his presence so urgently. It was not his first time at the mansion, but usually, on social visits. The office was the place to carry out business deals. He rang the bell, and a uniformed maid led him through the luxuriously decorated rooms and into the backyard where the DB Corp. president and another individual were chatting and having some drinks under a canopy. Mr. Brackman signaled him to join.

"Antoni, thank you for coming on short notice," he said, then he looked at the maid. "Please bring Mr. Kowalski a drink."

"Thank you, Mr. Brackman. I have to say I am a little puzzled by this urgent call. The wage negotiations are still a few months off."

"Yes, they are. And don't worry; when the time

comes, I will take good care of you as always. This conversation relates to a different matter. Let me introduce you to Joe Brown, our corporate security manager." Both men shook hands.

"Mr. Brackman, I am more intrigued now. Is there an issue with any of our union members?"

Joe smiled but remained silent as the two men continued the dialogue.

"No. It is not a problem with any of the workers at the brewery, but we have a problem with one individual."

Antoni crossed his arms. "I'm listening."

"The PNA has been after us about our waste-water's quality and claims that we are polluting the river." His face flushed while pointing his finger. "We have been operating this brewery for more than eighty years, and now they say that we're killing the fish."

Antoni was not known for his patience. "Mr. Brackman, I still do not see how this is a union problem. What can I do to help?"

"The union will have a problem if we can't stop this aggressive campaign." Don slammed his fist onto the table but then realized that his guest was uncomfortable and lowered his voice. "Sorry, it's not personal with you or the union. I called you because if we can't stop this and we are mandated to invest millions of dollars immediately or pay high fines, it will force us to cut costs." And he paused to gauge the impact of his words because he knew that Antoni understood that cutting costs would probably result in a workforce reduction.

"I see your concern now," Antoni leaned forward, "and how can we help?"

"I knew you would understand. The issue is not precisely the PNA but one individual within the PNA who is stirring the pot and leading others to confront us."

"And do you need some help to *convince* this individual that he should not put his nose where it doesn't belong?"

"Exactly. We can't do it ourselves because it could worsen our position and get us accused of intimidation, but I know sometimes you have to convince people to do certain things and are good at that." Brackman made steady eye contact and raised his eyebrows.

Antoni did not blink. "We're not criminals, but we have indeed been successful when we needed to persuade someone."

"Great. I'm glad we understand each other." Don nodded and looked at Joe. "Why don't you share with Antoni the information you found about Matt Hernandez?"

"Matt is a teacher at Lakeview School and a member of the PNA. He's taking a radical position against our company and ignored the explanations provided by our PR manager concerning the wastewater project, saying to his colleagues at the PNA that we have been lying to gain time since the company does not intend to comply with the regulations. He went further, and despite having his action plan to organize protests rejected, proceeded to go last night and take water samples from the river just downstream from our fences."

"I see you have quite an enemy, Mr. Blackman."

Don looked at him. "*We* have an enemy, Antoni."

The union leader pretended to ignore the remark. "I see the potential damage and think we can help. Do you have any additional information on Mr. Hernandez?"

Brackman nodded, and Joe continued, "We have been able to find some personal information. Hernandez is dating the daughter of one of our lawyers and has a group of friends that like to go skiing."

"Can't you ask your lawyer to help?" Antoni knew the probable answer but asked anyway.

"I intend to follow up with him but would like to use more direct methods."

"Understood. Anything else on possible weak spots of this individual?"

Joe had a tight-lipped smile. "We do. Hernandez's family lives in south Texas, near the border. That's where he grew up, and his parents and two siblings are still around. What's interesting is that his mother has not applied for citizenship like the rest of the family. She's so proud of her Mexican roots that she did not want to accept his son's offer to sponsor her to become a US citizen."

Antoni threw his head back and exhaled. "That is interesting and could help us but let's first work on the individual. Let me look into this, and we'll take some action soon. I believe you will not be worried again about Mr. Hernandez roaming around your brewery."

Don stood up, smiling, and stretched out his hand. "Antoni, I knew you would help, and I'll not forget it."

The men shook hands, and Antoni left.

"What do you think, Joe? Is he going to be able to do something?"

"I'm sure he will, Mr. Brackman. It was smart to mention the potential for job losses if this impacts the brewery."

ON THE FOLLOWING day, Jessica met with her father, Frank, and Tyler at the law firm.

"Did you talk to Matt?" her father asked while all eyes were on her.

She looked down briefly. "Yes, I did."

"And did you convince him that he could be in trouble if he continues with his behavior?" Tyler raised his voice.

"What kind of trouble are you talking about?" Jessica sneered.

John raised his hand. "Okay, stop the discussion and let Jessica update us on her conversation."

"Matt is convinced that DB Corp. is manipulating the system to avoid complying with the wastewater regulations, or at least delaying it as much as possible."

Frank kept a firm gaze on her. "And why is that?"

"Because he thinks they have some connections with the authorities that allowed them the first extension and are now delaying the response to the petition for a second extension that we have presented on their behalf."

John and Frank exchanged a glance.

"Furthermore, he suspects that Brackman is managing the PNA through its president, Peterson, who he believes is just a puppet."

Tyler rolled his eyes. "It looks like he has imagined a full conspiracy theory."

Jessica ignored him. "Matt also feels that Peterson spies on him. Nobody knew they were going to take a water sample last night except him and two friends and one of them made an excuse not to go. He must have been the one who alerted Peterson, who passed the information to Brackman and then to you. Matt is wondering why there's so much attention and urgency."

"Did you ask him whether we could help him understand the situation if he talks to us?"

"Yes, I did, and he thinks the firm would follow

the same line as DB Corp. He offered to share the information they have in terms of deviation from the wastewater regulations limits and the impact on marine life and jobs."

"How generous of him." Tyler smirked. "He wants to educate *us* on his environmental fables."

"I don't believe we need to hear his story now." Frank's tone was serious. "Why don't you two let John and I discuss this topic further?" Jessica and Tyler reluctantly left the room, and he continued, "It looks like this is a smart guy."

John scratched his head. "We may have a problem here, and the question is how to manage it. Did Brackman ask for anything specific from us?"

"No, he didn't. He just wanted to share so we're ready to act as needed."

"So far, it looks like a PR issue. Didn't we ask Jessica to put the priority on a plan?"

"Yes, and I'll ask Tyler to do some research on Matt Hernandez."

The two partners went to their offices, and Frank called his son. "I want you to follow this guy, Hernandez, and find out what else he's doing."

"Should we prepare a case against him for interfering with DB Corp. operations?" Tyler was fidgeting with his watch.

"No, it's too soon since we don't have anything to accuse him of doing. That's why I want you to find out what's going on and who he's talking to, so we may get some evidence to use against him. Keep it confidential and report your findings directly to me."

"I thought you would share the information with John."

"I will at the appropriate time, but since his daughter is dating Hernandez, I don't want to risk that relationship interfering with the investigation."

"Okay. Understood."

Frank smirked. "I thought you would be interested in finding some dirt on this guy, considering how you look at Jessica."

MATT WAS HAVING a cup of coffee at a trendy place in Pioneer Square when he saw Josh coming with a beautiful woman who was making heads turn with her long, black hair, sparkling blue eyes, contrasting olive skin, and a mischievous smile. When they approached his table, he stood up awkwardly and spilled his coffee. That generated a soft giggle from her while Josh made the introduction.

"Matt, this is my friend Rachel, the person I mentioned who works on Channel 5 and is willing to help us."

"Nice meeting you, Rachel, and thank you for being open to a discussion. I think I've seen you on the news."

She sat and tossed her hair. "Yes, I work for the

news team, usually as a street reporter. Josh told me about your quarrel with the brewery, and I'd like to learn more."

They ordered, and while waiting for the beverages, Matt shared a summary of the situation. "Do you think that we could get some coverage from your channel?"

"I believe the story could be appealing, but it needs some more concrete evidence of wrongdoing. I will bring it to our news director, who decides on whether to investigate potential stories."

Josh took a phone call, and when finished, stood up. "If you'll excuse me, I need to leave and see my father while you continue the conversation.'

Matt arched his eyebrows. "Anything wrong?"

"No. My dad called me because he had a chat with his friends, the fishermen, and wants to share what he heard."

"Do you want me to go with you?"

"I don't think it's necessary. You better stay with Rachel and plan the next step. Tomorrow I'll update you on whatever my father learned."

Josh left, and Rachel stared at Matt. "You don't remember me, do you?"

Matt moved back in his chair and tilted his head. "Have we met before? I doubt I would forget someone like you," he said, cheeks burning.

"More than ten years ago… does Mc Allen, Texas, sound familiar?"

His eyes opened, and pointing at her, he said, "Those eyes seemed familiar, but I couldn't place you. *Rachel Avila?*"

She chuckled and nodded. "Yes. We were neighbors, and then we moved because my dad got a job in Houston. I studied communications there, and after graduation, I got this job opportunity. I remember having a crush on you. At fourteen years old, I saw you as a mature man of seventeen—an unreachable dream."

"I can't believe that such a tiny teenager with braided hair could turn into such a beautiful woman."

She smiled and leaned on the table, reaching for his hand. "I never thought I would see you again."

He had trouble maintaining eye contact and looked down, mumbling, "I have a girlfriend, and we're getting married soon."

She maintained her hand on his. "Congratulations. I'm happy for you and wish you the best."

He felt more relaxed, and they continued talking for a while, laughing and bringing back all memories from their youth.

JESSICA WAS READY to have dinner with her parents when she received a phone message with a video.

"Guess where your boyfriend is right now."

The screen showed Matt holding hands and

laughing with a beautiful young woman in a *café*. She immediately walked away from the table.

"What happened, Jessica?" Her mother was puzzled but knew that her daughter had just received some bad news.

"Nothing. I am going to my room. I need some privacy." Her misty eyes and a tone of irritation in her voice gave away how she felt.

As soon as she was alone, Jessica called Matt, but he didn't answer. Then she looked again at the message and noticed Tyler had sent it.

"Tyler, where did you take that video? Is it real?"

"I would love to say that it's not, but your boyfriend is having a good time with that gorgeous woman." He was enjoying the conversation and imagining Jessica's face hearing the news about Matt's cheating.

"And how did you know they were in that café?"

"I followed Matt to try to figure out what he's up to with the complaints about DB Corp. He was sitting at a table, and his friend Josh showed up with the woman, but after a few minutes, Josh left, leaving Matt and the girl alone. I don't know what they have been talking about, but it is obvious they are having fun."

"What do you mean having fun? Are they still together?"

"Yes. I am outside the café, but I can see them

through one of the windows. The encounter has been going on for more than one hour."

"That's *why* he's not answering my call," Jessica raised her voice.

He tried to hide his satisfaction with the turn of events. "Wow. That is not a good sign. Sorry, Jessica."

"Give me the address," she demanded." I want to see it myself."

"I don't know if that would be a good idea. Maybe you should calm down first and get an explanation from Matt later. I'm sure he would be able to explain it." Tyler tried to sound sympathetic but added fuel to the fire.

"I will see you there." She hung up.

It took her about thirty minutes to find the place, and after parking her car, Jessica barged inside. She could not see Matt but noticed Tyler waving at her.

"Where are they?" Jessica's face flushed, and her eyebrows lowered.

"Just left about ten minutes ago. I was going to follow them but decided to wait for you since you may need some help to confront this situation."

"This can't be happening." She fought tears. "There has to be an explanation."

"I am sure there is one." He steepled his fingers and considered his statement but then shook his head. "But why is he not answering your calls?"

She began sobbing.

"Please, Jessica," he caught her hand, "don't imagine the worst. I'm here to help with whatever you need."

"Thank you, Tyler. I know I can count on you."

"Have you eaten anything?"

"No. I was ready to have dinner with my parents when I got your message."

"Oh, I'm so sorry. Let me invite you for dinner to apologize for my mistake," he said and kissed Jessica's hand.

"There is no need to apologize. In any case, you were trying to help as a friend."

"That's exactly right. I always wish the best for you, even if I need to share some not-so-good news. But, if it'll make you feel better, let's order some dinner. I heard this place has some great steaks."

"Okay," she agreed with a half-smile on her face, "I can't refuse your invitation. I need someone to talk about this."

"And I will always be here for you. Waiter, please bring us a menu."

AT THE WALTONS' residence, Mary wasn't too happy with the report from her friend, Michelle, from the PTA meeting.

"She heard the questions about Matt's capabilities that we prepared with Amy but wouldn't budge one inch. She very politely heard our concerns and promised to monitor his performance but confirmed that she's confident that Matt will do a great job."

Mary's voice couldn't hide how she felt. "I don't know what Mrs. Douglas sees in him. We'll need to step up the pressure."

Chapter 7

MATT GOT OUT of bed and was ready to have some breakfast when the doorbell rang. As soon as he opened, Josh rushed in, gesticulating. "Good news, bro. I have some *good* news."

"Good morning to you, too," Matt yawned.

"Sorry. As I told you, I went to see my dad last night, and he got something for us."

"What is it?" His friend's excitement was beginning to speed up his brain.

"Remember that my dad told us that he would probably be able to introduce us to some of the fishermen?"

"Yes, and that would probably be helpful to understand the impact of the wastewater contamination."

"He decided to go talk to them and learned a few things."

"C'mon, just tell me what it is. I'm listening."

"They are scared because their association is not helping them."

There was a tight-lipped smile on Matt's face. "It certainly sounds familiar."

"Yes, they think that DB Corp. bought their association leader, and he's not supporting any action against the brewery."

"That is not good news. What are you so excited about?"

"Because one of the fishermen my dad knows has a friend who used to work at the brewery for more than twenty years. He told my dad a story about a big fire that destroyed part of the brewery around fifteen years ago."

"And is that something that could help us now?"

Josh was walking with one hand on his hips and the other pointing up. "Apparently, DB Corp. successfully hid any evidence on the cause of the fire. The fire not only caused material damage but also took nine lives."

"I didn't know that beer manufacturing could be that dangerous." Matt's brow creased. "Wait, a fire? Remember Brian's last words to his sister? *Matt, the fire,* I bet he was trying to tell us something about what he had found and thought was so important."

"Precisely. And that was why we need to talk with this guy. We need to learn more about his experience, that incident, and the brewery operation."

Matt nodded quickly. "Agreed. And we can also

learn whether they have been using undue influence to hide things since that time. When can we go?"

"I think we can go now. It's early, and being Saturday, we may have a chance to catch him."

"Okay. Let's head out then."

"Wait," Josh caught his friend's arm, "didn't Jessica organize a ski trip today?"

"Oh, yeah, but if we get back by late morning, we still can go skiing. I'll try to call her from the car. I haven't talked to her since yesterday anyway."

THEY JUMPED INTO Josh's truck and took the freeway, leaving town in the same general direction as the brewery. Most workers lived in a couple of suburbs that had grown in population throughout the years as the plant had expanded its operations. They were chatting while driving over the mountains and enjoying the river's gorgeous view meandering toward the ocean. Josh raised his right hand from the wheel and touched his temple.

"I forgot to mention that the lab technician called me and said the results of the water analysis are ready.

Matt turned his head with his eyes wide open. "What does it say? Do you have them?"

"He'll send it to me today but mentioned that the levels of BODs and TSS are very high."

"And what does it mean?"

"BOD measures the level of oxygen that it takes to degrade organic matter. When it's high, it can damage marine life. TSS measures total suspended solids, and a high number also indicates trouble for aquatic life."

"Therefore, the impact the fishermen see could be the result of the poorly treated wastewater." Matt hit the dashboard with his fist and sounded as enthusiastic as a child on Christmas day.

"Wait, remember the technician told us that a single sample is not proof of anything. The regulations call for weekly and monthly averages."

"Okay, but this is an indication in the right direction." Matt could not hide his excitement.

Josh tried to temper his friend's euphoria. "Look, we're getting closer."

They turned onto a secondary road that led to the town of Miscales, population 1,560 inhabitants, as a carved wooden sign proudly announced on one side of the road. They stopped to ask for directions and finally arrived at an old but well-maintained house. A small front yard with carefully arranged flower beds and a couple of perfectly pruned bushes showed that someone was spending time to take care of it. The right job for a retired person. Matt and Josh went through a small gate and rang the bell.

"Mr. Mario Ramirez?" Josh extended his hand to a smiling man in his sixties.

"Yes, that's me. Just call me Mario."

"I'm Josh Miller, and this is my friend, Matt. We got your name from a friend of my father. Did he call you about our visit?"

"Got a call last night and understand you're interested in knowing more about the big fire at the brewery."

"We would appreciate it if you could share the story and some details about the plant operation since we understand you worked there for several years."

"Come in, and I'll tell you what I know."

They sat around a kitchen table where Mario had already placed a box with some photos and documents. He offered them coffee and homemade cookies.

"Mario," Matt leaned forward, "not sure how much you know about our interest in the brewery operation but let me give you a summary." He shared the story about the wastewater conflict and their suspicion that the company management was hiding something and using all sorts of influences to avoid complying with existing regulations and then continued.

"We understand that there was a big fire more than fifteen years ago, and it's not clear what happened. We wonder why a relatively safe operation like a brewery would go through such a major incident. It doesn't seem to relate to the problem with the waste-water but wonder whether there is a pattern of trade of influences in the DB Corp. operations."

"That's what many people asked at that time. I was in maintenance and knew all parts of the brewery. The fire started with an explosion in a trailer used then as the laboratory and went quickly through the warehouse next door and the trucks that were being loaded that night for deliveries the next morning. It was a big mess, and lives were lost." Mario lowered his head and tried to hide some sad memories.

"A lab?"

"Yes, you know, for quality control and development of new blends."

"But what could cause an explosion in a lab that doesn't handle explosive or flammable materials?"

"There were no explanations. The official report was that an electrical short circuit initiated the fire, but not many people believed it. The media asked lots of questions and challenged the findings, but suddenly, nobody talked about it and the case was closed. I have some photos and newspaper clippings from that time that you may find useful." He pushed the box toward them.

Matt began looking at the content of the box, and Josh gazed at their host. "Mario, what do *you* think happened?"

The retired worker shook his head. "It is difficult to know, but there were rumors that some illegal operations were run in that lab."

Matt looked at Josh. "And what illegal operations could those be?"

"I could never confirm it and don't have any

proof." Mario crossed his arms and raised his sight into the ceiling.

"But you might suspect something. You can trust us," Josh insisted.

"I found it suspicious that the fire started at night since the technicians should have done all lab work during the day. The firefighter's first comments mentioned traces of flammable materials at the site, but the reports never suggested anything of the sort. After the incident, the company built a new lab with all sorts of safety features. I know because I saw it during construction."

"Do you think this lab is still used for something else?"

"Let's put it this way. A brewery operation has little flammable material except for dust clouds that form in the conveying, sieving, and milling malt grain processes. Dust collection systems extract those fumes. The other possible source would be ethanol formed at the end of the process, but beer is diluted to the point that it is not highly flammable."

"So, you're saying it's difficult to believe that a lab handling those products would require a very sophisticated safety system."

"There's something more. My curiosity led me to monitor the operations and found that the lab was working night hours regularly. Why would a simple quality control lab have to be open at night when the production ran during the day?"

"Those are excellent questions, Mario," Matt

nodded. "Did you ever share your concerns with anyone else?"

"I tried and was told that I shouldn't be thinking about conspiracy theories since it was just an unfortunate accident. A short time later, the company assigned me to a new plant area far away from the lab. Also, management warned all employees not to talk with the media about the fire to avoid *interfering with the investigation* as management put it."

Josh's eyebrows raised. "It sounds like they wanted to have absolute control over the information. How long did the investigation last?"

"Everything was fast. As I mentioned, there were questions during the first couple of days, but then the official report was published; the company made a substantial contribution to the families of those who died in the fire and vowed to rebuild the damaged facilities. In less than a week, the whole incident was no longer in the news."

Matt got up. "Okay, Mario, thanks for sharing. We may come back to chat some more if you don't mind."

"Any time. Be careful with what you are investigating. Those are rough people."

The two friends got into the truck and left Miscales. Josh was driving with his hands firmly grasping the wheel and his eyes fixated on the road, but his brain was processing the details of the conversation they'd just had with Mario. Matt had his eyes closed while playing with a pen between his fingers.

"Josh, what do you think?"

"It's obvious that something is going on in that brewery since their executives have built high-level relationships to protect them. It looks like it goes beyond normal PR for any industrial operation, but the question is, why?"

"I wonder if your friend, Rachel, could find out more about the fire and the media coverage."

Josh hit the wheel and looked at Matt. "That's a good idea. She wasn't working at Channel 5 at that time, but they should have the coverage files. I will ask her to do some research."

"Great. By the way, did you know Rachel and I grew up together in Texas?"

"Small world," he said, shaking his head.

"Yes. We spent some time yesterday talking about the past. Her family was living next door to ours until they moved out to Houston, and I never heard from her until you brought her to the restaurant."

"Remember you have a fiancée," Josh teased.

"She is beautiful and a wonderful person, but I have Jess now. *You* should go after her."

With a half-smile, he said, "I tried, but we're just friends. She gave me the *I'm not ready for a serious commitment yet,* which is a pity because I would go after a girl like her." Then he looked at Matt like mothers do when children forget about homework. "Don't you have to call Jessica to find out at what time we need to meet to go skiing?"

Matt stroke his forehead. "You're right. With all this excitement, I forgot about the plans for today." He called Jessica but looked at his friend with the corners of his mouth drawn downward. "She's not answering and didn't take my call last night, either."

"Have you done anything to her?"

"Not that I know of. I haven't talked to Jessica since the day before yesterday, and everything was fine. I shared what we have been doing, and she seemed to understand."

"Can you call her parents and ask about her?"

"Talking to her parents is not the best idea," Matt looked down. "They don't support our relationship."

"Think that you can gain some points by calling and showing that you are worried because you haven't heard from Jessica when trying to confirm a plan to go skiing today."

"You're right, my friend. I'll call now." Matt called the Daltons, and it was a short conversation. He turned to Josh with his eyes wide open. "Her mother said she already left for Crystal Mountain. Why would she leave without waiting for us?"

"Not sure, but let's go by your place, pick up the ski equipment, and head to Crystal Mountain to find out.

Chapter 8

DON BRACKMAN WAS enjoying a snack at the end of an eighteen-hole golf game. He was in a good mood and still bragging about his six birdies when his phone rang. After checking the caller ID, he ignored it.

"No business today," he proclaimed with a big smile and raised a beer mug that his partners followed, eager to celebrate the unusual cheerful state of mind of the boss.

The Saturday golf games were an opportunity to be close to the chief, and nobody would spoil it by contradicting him or making a comment that could mean losing their job. When a second call came in, and Don Brackman frowned, everybody knew the good times were over. He excused himself and walked away from the table to take the call.

"Mr. Brackman, this is Antoni Kowalski."

"You better have something important to say because you're interrupting my golf outing."

"Sorry, sir, but I think you should know this."

"What is it?"

"We followed Hernandez early this morning. He went to Miscales with a friend and visited a former brewery employee, Mario Ramirez."

"I think I remember that name."

"He was the maintenance guy who began to sniff around after the fire and asked too many questions."

Don Brackman nodded. "Yes, the same one we moved to a new job at the mill room, far away from the lab."

"The one we convinced a few years later to take early retirement, receiving a hefty severance package."

"Why would Matt Hernandez want to talk to that guy?"

"We visited with Ramirez after they left and reminded him about the nice retirement package he got from the company. We also explained to him that Mr. Hernandez and his friend were trying to use the banner of the green movement to force some investments in new equipment that would result in the loss of many jobs."

"Good story and clever on your part to try to win his support. Did he buy it?"

"At the very least, we put some doubt in his mind about Hernandez's intentions and at the same time reminded him what the company has done for him.

Hopefully, he feels that he owes some loyalty to his old employer and his fellow workers."

"Do you think he could be a threat to us?"

"I don't think so, and anyway, he doesn't know anything and only has some unanswered questions in his mind."

"Okay, Antoni. I understand Ramirez is under control, but this event worries me, considering Matt Hernandez's actions. Keep a close eye on him and do not hesitate in giving him a warning about not getting into trouble."

Don Brackman rejoined the group, but everybody noticed his mood had changed when he announced, "The outing is over. I'm going home."

All the laughter stopped, and the only sound was that of chairs moving out of the way and some low voice comments while walking toward the parking area.

JOSH AND MATT left the city driving on I-5 south. Some cotton-like clouds added silhouettes of monsters and cute animals to the blue sky. It was a chilly day, and the roads were crowded after a front brought powdered snow to the delight of weekenders searching for the slopes' enchantment. They were planning to arrive in time for the usual lunch at the Mountain Café to catch up with friends.

The conversation was light and cheerful as they were trying to purposely focus on enjoying the day after a busy and troublesome week. Close to noon, the first noticeable amounts of snow on the side of the road indicated that they were close to their destination, and about forty-five minutes later, they entered one of the spacious parking lots at the base of the mountain.

"This is the part I hate about skiing," Josh was fighting to keep balance while walking in ski boots.

A group of teenagers did not seem to share his concern as they moved quickly, chatting out loud to compensate for the "click-clock" of their boots hitting the pavement.

"There's Jessica." Matt's eyes beaming happiness, soon turned into a frown. "Who's with her?"

"It's a little far, and I can't see the guy." Josh made a visor with his hand over his eyes to protect them from the glare.

Matt waved at Jessica but did not get a reply. "Do you think she didn't see me?"

"She was looking this way, so I wouldn't know why she would not have seen you."

"Exactly. What is going on?"

"Not sure, but you'll find out in a couple of minutes."

Jessica and Tyler were chatting at an outside table when they approached.

"Hi, Jess," Matt said with a worried smile on his face.

She looked up as if surprised by his presence. "Hello."

Tyler gazed at him but did not say a word. He instead extended his hand to Jessica. "We're done with lunch. Should we go back to the slopes?"

Matt got closer to Tyler with fire in his eyes but turned to her. "I don't know what's going on, but I haven't heard from you since Thursday. You aren't taking my calls, and now I find you with this despicable individual who is trying to steal *my* girl."

Tyler got up, and his eyes met Matt's a couple of inches apart. "If this were *my* girl, I would take better care of her."

"Wait," Jessica shouted, "I am not the property of anybody and will not tolerate any violence here."

They refrained from hitting each other and looked at her like siblings scolded by their mother for fighting.

"You, Matt Hernandez," her cheeks reddened, and brows furrowed, "do not have the right to complain about my not taking your calls. I called you last night, and you didn't answer."

"Is that what this is all about? My battery was dead, and I called you when I got home, but you didn't answer. I can't believe you're behaving like this over such a minor issue."

"No. I didn't respond to a minor issue. I reacted

to *this*." Taking her phone, she showed Matt the video with him and Rachel.

He gasped, and his arms shoot up but then smiled at her. "I see why you got upset, but I can easily explain that."

"Now come the stories to cover up what's obvious." Tyler rolled his eyes and shook his head while sitting down with crossed arms.

Matt ignored him. "I don't know how you got that video and pictures, but I can imagine." He threw an icy look at Tyler. Then, softening his voice, said, "That woman in the picture is Rachel Avila, someone I just saw yesterday after more than ten years without knowing where she was. We grew up together in south Texas, and our families were close. Then they moved out to Houston and we lost track of each other until yesterday when Josh brought her to a meeting. She works at Channel 5 and agreed to help us with the DB Corp. wastewater issue."

Josh was quietly observing the drama but quickly added, "That's true, Jessica. I introduced, or I thought I was introducing Rachel to Matt because I have known her for some time now. But I had no idea they grew up together."

She looked down, her fingers tapping the table as if the rhythmic noise on the wood would help to put her thoughts in order.

"Surely, you don't believe those lies." Tyler's face flushed, and his finger pointed to Matt. "He tells you a story, and his best friend confirms it. *How convenient*. And how about the smiles and hugs?"

"We were just so happy to get together again and share stories from our childhood that we laughed and enjoyed the moment. We hugged because it is common in Hispanic culture to express affection."

"Yeah, yeah, yeah, do you express your affection to everybody or just beautiful women like your alleged *friend*?"

Matt could not control himself, grabbed Tyler by his shirt collar, and pulled him up from the chair. Before Tyler could retaliate, a right hand crushed his jaw and sent him to the floor.

"*No*." Jessica stood up quickly and positioned herself between the two men to prevent an escalation of the fight. "I heard your explanation Matt, and if I didn't know you, I would have doubts about the explanation." Then she turned to Tyler with a cold gaze. "I believe you created all this on purpose. You mentioned your interest in me to my mother, but I'm not a child dazzled by tricks, nor a fool deceived by intrigues. You conquer the heart of a woman by understanding her feelings and making her happy, not by trying to destroy her heart." Then she looked at Matt and Josh. "You two still have a lot of explaining to do and details to tell, but why don't we go enjoy that fresh powder?" Her bright smile was sunshine to Matt's eyes.

Tyler touched his chin while walking away to get

his snowboard but turned around and yelled. "This is not going to end like this."

Matt began to go after him, but she caught his arm. "It's not worth it. Let him go while you tell me more about your friend."

They stood at the table, and Matt and Josh brought Jessica up to speed on who Rachel was and how she was planning to help them. Jessica, with her lips tight and eyes narrowed, did not say a word.

Matt swallowed. "Something wrong?"

"Is she pretty?"

"I would say yes," his head tilted, "but what does it have to do with what I told you?"

She could not contain herself and laughed. "You're so adorable." Then she hugged him.

Matt shrugged and opened his hands while looking at Josh, who was standing behind her. "I'm sure I am, but I don't understand whether this means you're not mad anymore."

She had the sweetest sparkle in her eyes. "The way you told the story can't leave room for any doubt, and I love you because I see through your eyes that you're happy to have found an old friend." Jessica put a hand on his chest and puckered her lips. "But I have a request."

"What is it?" he babbled defenselessly under such masterful play of female power.

"That I get to know your friend. Why don't we get together tomorrow?"

"That's a great idea. I'm sure Josh will be happy to call Rachel and invite her," he winked to his friend.

"What does that mean?"

Josh's cheeks flushed. "Matt's just kidding."

"Can you believe our friend here likes Rachel but is afraid that she may reject him?"

She giggled. "C'mon, Josh. We'll help you win her heart. I'll let you know if she is right for you when I meet her tomorrow."

"Good deal. I need to do some skiing now." Matt led the way toward the ski racks next to the café.

They went to the gondola and spent the rest of the afternoon running the slopes and enjoying the fresh snow.

After three hours and being back at the bottom of the mountain, Jessica lifted her goggles, planted her poles, and had a big smile on her face. "It's been a blast, but I'm ready for some hot chocolate."

"Don't you want to go for the last run? Now is the best time because most people have gone home. Please?" Matt pleaded like a child wanting a last piece of candy.

She smiled. "I know you like to go enjoy the peace of the slopes when the sun is going down, but I'm tired. Why don't you go, and I'll wait here at the café?"

"Are you sure?"

"*Yes.* Go."

"I don't want to leave you alone with Tyler around."

Josh grinned. "I'll stay with her, and don't worry about Tyler because I saw him going to the gondola when we got here, so he must be on the slopes."

"Love you." Matt blew a kiss at his love.

JESSICA AND JOSH found a table with a good view and began chatting while Matt headed toward the slopes. There was usually a line to get to the eight-passenger gondola, but at that late time, he just went straight in with only two other skiers who were chatting and laughing about their adventures of the day.

The ride to the summit took twelve minutes, and Matt enjoyed the view of the pines covered with a thick, white blanket as the cabin was climbing toward the summit. Close to the mountain's top, the branches bent as if tired of holding such a heavy load, but the trees stood like giants, guarding the slopes for the skiers.

When they reached the top, he got out and took a couple of minutes to appreciate the fantastic view. Matt was so focused on admiring the white peaks and the green hillsides that he didn't notice someone hiding behind the ski-patrol shack. Matt adjusted his goggles and began a slow descent. Without a crowd of skiers around, he could feel the silence and peace that made these late runs the highlight of the day.

His skies swooshed, turning in smooth curves, producing a rhythmic sound like soft music that soothed his soul. He heard the typical "on your left" warning that indicates another skier is coming on your left side. He stayed on the right while the other skier moved ahead but then reduced his or her speed. That seemed strange, and Matt was ready to pass the skier when he heard another voice, "on your left." Matt adjusted his speed, but now the second skier stayed on his left, and he found himself without a choice on where to go except following them. He could not stop without risking a dangerous fall.

He tried to stay calm, but his adrenaline rose, and his brain was working full speed, trying to understand what was going on. The two skiers did not say a word, but it was evident that they worked together and led him toward the slope's right edge. He focused on not falling but could not avoid remembering Mario Ramirez's comment from that morning. "*Be careful with what you are investigating. Those are rough people,*" and a chill run down his spine. He tried to slow down, but they would do the same, and it looked like they were a perfectly synchronized three-man team except that he did not volunteer for it.

They were getting close to a fork in the slope where Matt would usually take a left at a blue-rated route when enjoying a peaceful run, but the two men led him toward the right on a more difficult, black slope. He braced for a more dangerous experience when they began going down the more challenging path, but after a couple of minutes, the skier on his left shouted, "*Relax. This has just been a warning,*" and sped away, followed by his partner.

Matt opened his mouth but couldn't say a word because suddenly a snowboarder came close to him, sliding sideways and creating a cloud of powdered snow that hit him in a wave, blinding him. The surprising departure of the two skiers, plus this snowboarder's reckless behavior, made him lose control. He went into the brushes, lost a pole in a tree branch, and saw a big tree coming to him at high speed.

"*Oh my God,*" and everything went black.

Chapter 9

JESSICA LOOKED AT her watch. "Shouldn't he be back by now?"

"He'll be here in a few minutes. You know he especially enjoys that last run and takes his time coming down."

"You're right. By the way, why did Matt say that you like Rachel but are afraid she may reject you?"

Josh lowered his gaze and played with a napkin. "Some time ago, I suggested that I was interested in her, and she mentioned that she was happy we're good friends."

She smiled and shook her head. "Why are men such cowards?"

He raised his eyebrow, but she continued, "You said you *suggested* having an interest in her. What did you say? Why not tell her your feelings? If she told you that she is happy about being your friend, maybe she opened a door for you rather than closing it for a romantic relationship."

Josh's eyes brightened. "Do you think so?"

"It is a possibility, but unless you take the first step, you won't know."

"Thanks, Jessica. You're a good friend."

"Just trying to help. But I'm beginning to get worried since it's getting dark and I don't see any more skiers coming down the mountain."

"Yeah, he should have been here by now. Let's ask that guy in the ski patrol uniform if there are still people on the mountain."

They got up and walked in the direction of a man coming toward them with his skis on his shoulder.

"Excuse me, sir. We've been waiting for our friend who went for a late run, but we're beginning to get concerned because he isn't back yet."

The patrolman looked at them with sad eyes. "There was an accident on one of the black slopes. Someone hit a tree, and we found him when doing our last run."

"Oh no," Jessica screamed.

"Calm down; maybe it's someone else," Josh tried to provide support with a trembling voice.

"He was wearing a blue parka and black pants and found some documents under the name of Matthew Hernandez. Is he your friend?"

Then she began crying. "Yes, it's Matt." She took the patrolman by his arm. "Is he okay?"

"We found him unconscious. The first evaluation revealed that he suffered a concussion and a possible skull fracture. Hence, a couple of my colleagues brought him down to the emergency clinic to run some tests. I can take you there."

"Please."

They walked a few blocks to the village's emergency room located in a white building. The patrolmen identified Jessica and Josh as friends of the victim brought in a few minutes ago and guided them to a waiting room. Josh was holding Jessica by the shoulder while she was trying to clear her tears with a tissue. A doctor came soon after that.

"Are you family of the person who was involved in the accident?"

"I am his fiancée, and this is his best friend. Can you tell me how he's doing?"

"I'm afraid that he had a serious accident and we've already called the lifesaver helicopter to take him to the hospital in town. We don't have the equipment here to address his situation."

Jessica's shoulders slumped, and she covered her face with her hands. "Is he conscious now?"

"I'm afraid not. We are giving some medicine to stabilize him, but the sooner he gets to the hospital, the better. One of you can ride with him in the helicopter if you want. It is going to be leaving in a few minutes."

"Thank you, Doctor. I'll go with him." Suddenly Jessica turned despair into strength and looked at Josh. "He needs us to be strong so we can help. I'll see you at the hospital."

"I'm leaving right now and should be in town in a couple of hours. Take care. Matt's going to be fine."

When Jessica saw Matt on the stretcher, she remembered the kiss he had blown at her and the "*love you*" he had pronounced when heading toward the gondola that afternoon. Why had such a happy moment turned into this horror? She quickly dismissed any further thoughts and held his cold hand while walking to the helicopter. The big bird was waiting with its giant propeller purring and the blinking red and green navigation lights rivaling the sun's colorful display falling behind the snowed peaks of the mountains. In a few minutes, they took off, and she kept repeating, "*I'm here, and you're going to be okay,*" to an unconscious body that she felt somehow would hear her voice.

Josh went to his truck and was ready to drive a mad race to town when he realized that he was too stressed to drive and decided to take a few minutes to recover. He still couldn't believe that Matt, being such an avid skier, could have had such a terrible accident. The more Josh thought about it, the more he found himself looking for answers. He exhaled, grabbed the wheel, and shook his head. *There must be an explanation.* He got out of the car, went back to the emergency room, and asked where he could find the ski patrol office. It happened to be in an adjacent building, so he ran there, hoping to catch someone before leaving for the day.

The door was unlocked, and the same ski patrol

individual they had talked to earlier was collecting his belonging to wrap up the day.

"Excuse me. I know it is late, but can I talk to you for a minute?"

"Of course. You're the friend of the guy who had the accident today, right?. How is he doing?"

"The helicopter took him to the hospital in town, but I have something else I would like to talk about."

"Hope he gets better. It looks like it was a hard crash against that tree. What can I do for you?"

"Matt's an excellent skier, and I can't believe he could have had such an accident, especially late in the day. He enjoys that last run because he wants to appreciate the scenery and the peace of being alone coming down the mountain. I've gone with him sometimes on those late runs, and he doesn't take any risks."

The patrolman kept eye contact and leaned forward. "I've seen many accidents sometimes caused by a distraction. He was doing one of the black slopes, so it seems he was enjoying the challenge of a difficult run."

Josh raised his eyebrows. "You see, that's another piece of information that doesn't fit. He would never take the most difficult slopes because it would prevent him from enjoying the surrounding environment."

"Was he in good health? We have seen cases of people crashing because of fainting or having a heart problem."

"That is very improbable because he is a very healthy individual."

The guy shrugged. "I see your concerns but don't know what to say."

"Can you do a thorough investigation of the accident? Are there cameras that could provide some leads?"

"There are webcams at the top near the gondola station and few other key areas, but if you have any suspicion of foul play, I suggest you go to the police. The ski patrol doesn't have the training or capabilities to run an investigation. Our role is to protect the skiers, provide first aid, and in cases like this, report what we have seen."

"I understand. I'd like to get the police involved."

The patrolmen nodded. "As you wish. We'll provide all the information we have if they ask for it. You can go to the sheriff's office at the entrance to the village, and they'll tell you how to proceed."

They shook hands, and Josh went back to his truck. He made a stop to file a police report, and the officer took note of his declaration.

"Unfortunately, this is a rather typical accident around here. Are you suggesting that someone may have caused your friend's incident?" The officer stared at him.

"I'm only saying that it's very suspicious that an excellent skier going for a slow and enjoyable run would end up hitting a tree on a difficult slope." Josh kept looking at the officer.

"Does he have any enemies or someone you think may want to hurt him?"

"Don't know of enemies, but we are involved in an investigation for violation of environmental regulations and have been warned to be careful about what we're getting in."

"And who told you that?"

"Prefer not to reveal the name because if this is dangerous, that person may be in harm's way."

"Okay. I understand your concern. Let me see what we can do."

Josh left with the impression that the officer did not share the importance of the investigation. Anyway, there wasn't too much else to do, and he decided to continue his drive into town to find out how Matt was doing.

THE HELICOPTER'S FLIGHT took about twenty-five minutes and, as soon as they landed, a team of medical personnel took Matt on a stretcher to the ICU. The hospital's staff told Jessica to wait in a small room with a few chairs and a small couch lined up against the wall. She could not believe that two hours ago they were chatting so happily about a great day of skiing, and now, she got some tissues from her purse and tried to contain the tears that were beginning to flow and threatened to become an uncontrollable waterfall. She felt alone and didn't know what to do. Her parents didn't care about Matt and his family was far away. The only anchor point for her was Josh, but he was probably still driving from the mountain. She lowered her head and cupped it into her hands, letting out some soft sobs.

"Family of Matt Hernandez?" A man in his fifties, wearing the typical white coat, looked at her. He had an upright posture and a severe facial expression, but the way he talked gave her confidence.

"Yes. I'm his fiancée. Is he okay?" She held her breath and stood up.

"I'm Dr. Becker, Head of Neurosurgery at the hospital. I just wanted to give you a first report on the condition of Mr. Hernandez. He is still unconscious."

She shut her eyes.

"But he's stable. He has a linear fracture in the skull, and a CT scan showed some internal bleeding and brain tissue swelling. I understand he had an accident?"

"He was skiing, and the ski patrol found him. They said he hit a tree."

The doctor nodded. "It must have been a hard impact. That explains the extent of the damage. At this point, we have to wait while we run additional tests and closely monitor the evolution."

"Can I see him?"

"I would recommend waiting until morning.

Right now, he is sedated and, as I mentioned, unconscious."

"And what would be the next steps?"

"One concern is the swelling that can increase the pressure inside the skull and, if that happens, it could cause brain damage."

Jessica's eyes were wide open. "Does it mean that he may need brain surgery?"

"I know it sounds scary, but we may need to insert a small device through the skull that we connect to a monitor that provides a constant reading. That way, we can treat the swelling as needed. Miss Dalton, you tell me if this is too much information. I know it's difficult to digest while still in shock from the accident."

"It is okay, Doctor," her voice was firm even if she felt her legs shaking, "I want to know everything."

"The only additional information I have is that we are waiting to see if the blood clots dissolve."

"And what happens if they don't?"

"Then we'll have to eliminate them surgically."

Jessica's legs gave up, and she felt like fainting. The doctor held her, set her down onto the couch, and called a nurse who gave her some water. After a few minutes, she recovered and was breathing normally.

"Don't worry. You just had a normal body reaction to all the stress you went through today. We are doing all we can, and there is a good possibility for a full recovery if Matt reacts as we expect him to within the next forty-eight hours."

"When do you think he may wake up?"

"Not sure. Sometimes it takes a few hours and other times a few days. We must wait while keeping him under constant monitoring. You can go home and rest if you wish since we'll probably not have anything new to report until morning."

"Thank you, but I'll stay here. Please let me know any updates as soon as they're available."

Jessica had been pacing around the small room for more than one hour when the door opened, and finally, a familiar face showed up. She ran and hugged Josh as if he were a saving branch in the turbulent flow of emotions that had dragged her throughout the last few hours.

Chapter 10

THE NIGHT AT the hospital passed without any news while Jessica and Josh tried to take quick naps between conversations about the accident. They both agreed that what may have caused the accident was puzzling. Jessica called her parents to let them know about Matt's condition and was a little disappointed at her mom's calm behavior. Josh was leaving to get some coffee and muffins from the cafeteria when the doctor came.

"Good morning, Dr. Becker; anything new? How is he doing?" Jessica fired the questions while her right hand was twirling the ring on her left hand.

"He had a relatively good night considering the situation, but we have decided to take out the blood clot surgically by performing what it's called a neuro thrombectomy."

"Is that dangerous?" Josh's eyes were wide open.

The doctor put his hands over their shoulders and looked at them both. "Any surgery around the brain has its risks, but if we don't do anything, we may have a worse outcome like brain damage. It is a routine procedure, and we are confident that he will recover."

Jessica took the doctor's hand from her shoulder and held it between her two hands. Some tears rolled down her cheeks. "I trust you, Doctor. Please bring him back to us."

"I promise we'll do our best. It may take a few hours before we can give you any information, so try to relax to the extent possible and take care of yourselves."

When the doctor left, they didn't say a word. Jessica was sitting and quietly sobbing while Josh banged away his frustration against the wall with his fist. Finally, he turned to look at her.

"We need to go downstairs to the cafeteria and get out of this small room. Some fresh air would be good, and maybe we can walk a little. There is nothing to do here for a couple of hours."

She closed her eyes for a moment and took a deep breath. "You're right. We're not helping Matt by being here and need to be strong because he's going to need us. Let's go."

They got out of the hospital and walked through a small park. It was a gorgeous day, the dancing waters of a fountain, a few children running around, and the birds singing were signs that life continued, and they started to feel better. Josh mentioned to

Jessica that he had filed a report with the police, and she liked the idea.

"Did they say they would investigate?"

"They said they would look into it—whatever that means."

"We'll need to put some pressure on them to make it happen."

The conversation continued while going back to the cafeteria to keep waiting. Josh was ordering one coffee, one hot chocolate, and a couple of muffins when he heard a familiar voice.

"Josh, I've been looking for you."

He grinned while his voice sounded louder than he expected. "Rachel."

"How is Matt? What a *terrible* accident."

"He's been in the ICU, and the doctor said he's been stable during the night. Still unconscious, though. We're waiting for the result of an operation to remove a blood clot from his brain."

She covered her mouth with her hand and opened her eyes wide. "Oh no, it's worse than I thought."

Jessica looked and noticed the young woman talking to Josh and recognized who she was.

"Jessica, this is Rachel."

She took Jessica's hand between hers. "I'm sorry about your fiancé. I'm sure everything is going to be okay."

"Thank you, Rachel. I was looking forward to meeting you but not under these circumstances."

"Yes, same with me. I was happy when Josh texted me yesterday with the invitation to get together today. Then I saw his second text this morning and came as soon as I could. Matt used to be like a brother to me. If there's anything I can do to help, just ask."

"I heard a lot about you and appreciate your being here. We can help each other to overcome this situation." Jessica was instantly at ease with this beautiful woman who seemed to radiate warmth and sincerity. *No wonder Matt likes her so much,* she thought while staring at her sad blue eyes.

They sat around the table and shared anecdotes of their lives with Matt.

While holding her coffee mug, Rachel looked at Jessica's eyes. "How do you think it happened? It's difficult to understand how he could have had such a major accident."

"I was discussing that with Josh, and he filed a police report."

"Yes," Josh shrugged, "but I'm not sure whether they will investigate. The officer who took the information suggested there are a lot of similar accidents in the area."

Rachel stared at him. "Where did you file the report?"

"At the police station at the entrance of the Crystal Mountain Village."

Rachel's eyes brightened. "Oh, good. That's Crystal County, and the sheriff is Carl White."

"And?" Jessica tilted her head.

"Sheriff White is known for his unabated pursuit of justice. If he's interested in the case, he'll get to the bottom of it."

"And how can we get his interest?"

"That's my part. I've interviewed him before and will pay him a visit to find out more about the accident. I'll mention that I know Matt and that we have serious doubts about it being an accident."

"That would be awesome." Jessica smiled for the first time in the last twenty-four hours.

Josh was unable to sit still. "Should I go with you?"

"It's not necessary, and you better stay with Jessica. If I get his interest, we can coordinate a second visit, and then you can both go. Hopefully, Matt gets better, and maybe he can explain what happened."

They went back to the waiting room, and after thirty minutes, Dr. Becker came out of the OR.

Jessica held her breath. "How is he?"

"Relax, I believe the procedure was successful. Matt's still under the effects of the anesthesia."

Jessica covered her face with her hands and began sobbing while Josh took her by the shoulders and looked at the doctor's eyes. "Will he recover soon?"

"We need to give it some time, but normally, I would expect that he'd need to stay in the hospital for a few days. It may take a couple of days for him to regain consciousness. It's not always the case, but it could happen."

Jessica was biting her lip. "I understand, Doctor. Thank you. Can I see him?"

"In about one hour but for no more than a few minutes, please. He needs to rest and be monitored."

The doctor left, and the three friends stayed in the waiting room until a nurse came and invited Jessica back. She was hopeful based on what the doctor had said, but she couldn't avoid feeling overwhelmed when she saw Matt unconscious and connected to all the life support equipment. Softly, she touched his hand.

"Promise me that you're going to get better. I love you."

Jessica and Josh decided to take turns to stay close to Matt while Rachel scheduled a visit with Sheriff White.

JESSICA CALLED THE Lakeview School and asked to talk to Mrs. Douglas.

"Hello, Mrs. Douglas. My name is Jessica Dalton, Matt Hernandez's fiancée."

"Hi, Ms. Dalton. Matt has mentioned your name

and the plans to get married. Congratulations. What can I do for you?"

"Just calling to let you know that Matt had an accident over the weekend and is in ICU."

"Oh, no. We've been worried since he didn't come to school. How is he doing?"

"He went through surgery, and the doctors say he's recovering well, but he's still unconscious." Jessica's voice began to break.

"I'm so sorry. How did it happen?"

"We went to Crystal Mountain to ski with some friends, and he was doing his usual last run when the ski patrol found him and reported he crashed into a tree."

"What an *awful* accident."

"Yes, but we don't believe it was an accident. Matt's a great skier and doesn't take risks."

"Do you think that someone could have caused it?" Mrs. Douglas sounded alarmed.

"We don't know, but the police are investigating it."

"Excuse me for asking, but does Matt have enemies?"

"Not that we know of, except that he's working with the PNA, and sometimes it creates reactions. Why do you ask?"

"It seems to me that some people are going after him."

"Could you be more specific?"

"I told Matt that when I shared with the school board the news of his promotion, I was challenged on his credentials to get it, and last Friday, another lady at a PTA meeting did the same thing as if the two women were working together."

"And who would do that?"

"The person who questioned me at the board meeting was Mary Dalton."

"*My mom*?"

"I wasn't sure you were family, but she was the individual."

"And was she also present at the PTA meeting?"

"No. The lady leading the questioning of Matt's credentials at the PTA was Amy Fawler."

"*Amy Fawler*?"

"Do you know her?"

Jessica hesitated. "No, but the name sounds familiar." Anger was building in Jessica's voice. *That's one of my mom's best friends.*

"It looks like you and Matt need to have a conversation with your mother when he recovers. Anyway, you can tell him that neither of those comments changed my mind, and I believe he's the right person to lead our social studies department."

"Thank you, Mrs. Douglas. I'll tell him and let you know how he's doing in the next few days."

"Please do, and our prayers are with him for a quick recovery."

Chapter 11

THE BLUE VAN of Channel 5 caught the attention of a few passersby at the Crystal Mountain Village entrance. An attractive woman got out and entered the county sheriff's office, where she had arranged a visit with Sheriff White.

"Good morning, Sheriff. Thank you for accepting our request for a meeting on such short notice." Rachel extended her hand across his desk.

"Knowing how you work, I assume that this must be important," the sheriff shook her hand and sat back behind a small desk, inviting her to do the same on a chair across from him after moving aside a pile of documents. The room was small and had a sour cigar smell. "What can I do for you?"

"There was a ski accident on Saturday, and I happen to know Matt Hernandez, the person involved, as well as his fiancée and a close friend. We're all puzzled about how this could have happened to him."

"Ski accidents are common here, unfortunately. Sometimes it's a lack of experience, people trying to do more than their skill level would recommend, distractions, sudden sickness while skiing, you name it. We've seen it all. Why do you think that his case is unusual?"

"Because he's an excellent skier, in good health, and usually takes the last run of the day very calmly since he likes to enjoy the solitude of the slopes close to sunset. The accident happened on a black slope, and that is something he wouldn't do. On the last run, he would go down an easier blue slope."

"I see. But he could've decided to go faster this time—"

"Sorry to interrupt, but there is something else."

Now the sheriff leaned forward and stared at her.

"Matt Hernandez is active with the PNA, and he's been investigating the DB Corp. Brewery for irregularities in complying with wastewater regulations. Someone has mentioned to him and his friend, Josh Miller, that they may get into trouble for doing so. Also, a couple of months ago, Brian Oliver, a friend of theirs who was also a PNA member and actively investigating the brewery operations, died while jogging in a hit-and-run car accident."

Sheriff White blew out his cheeks. "The brewery? One of my first assignments as a young officer was to investigate a fire at that brewery around fifteen years ago, and the whole case was suspiciously closed. It was frustrating for our team since we thought there were still a couple of loose ends, but the top brass told us not to look anymore." He leaned back in his chair. "Let me look at the report from the ski patrol, and I'll get back to you."

"I appreciate it, Sheriff. If you want, next time, I can introduce you to Josh Miller and maybe Matt Hernandez if he recovers."

"It would help."

THAT AFTERNOON RACHEL went to the hospital, and Jessica was in the waiting room. "How is he doing?"

Jessica's eyes were swollen and staring into space, but she turned her head and pretended to smile, seeing Rachel. "The doctors say his vital signs are favorably evolving, but he's still unconscious."

Rachel sat by her side and held her hand. "He'll be okay. We have to trust the doctors, and you'll see that soon Matt will be chatting with you."

Jessica was looking down.

"And I have some good news. I talked to Sheriff White, and he'll look into Matt's case. He was involved in investigating the brewery fire several years ago and has been suspicious of how they got out of that so easily. When I explained that Matt and Josh were warned about the danger of digging too much into their operations, he got interested."

Jessica hugged her new friend. "Thank you,

Rachel. We need to find out what happened to Matt and seek justice if, as we think, someone caused his accident."

Josh was entering the room when he heard them. "That's great news. I'm concerned that someone is trying to hurt Matt."

"I have to share something with you," Jessica muttered and lowered her head.

"What is it? Don't worry. We'll get to the bottom of this." Josh tried to comfort her.

"I called the school this morning and talked to the principal to tell her about Matt's accident."

"Did she say something that upset you?"

"No, she's worried about Matt's condition but mentioned that someone might be trying to do things against him, trying to sabotage him."

"Maybe now we find a connection with the accident." Josh pumped his fist in the air. "What did she say?"

"Mrs. Douglas is puzzled because people are questioning her decision about promoting Matt."

Josh sighed. "But why is that unusual?"

"Because she was challenged at the school board and the PTA meetings with basically the same questions and coming from what looks like a coordinated approach."

"And who could be doing that?"

"*My mother.*"

"What? Why would your mother do that?"

"Matt told me that he suspected my mom went to the board meeting to speak against him. Mrs. Douglas didn't mention my mother's name to Matt, but now she has confirmed she was the person challenging his promotion. She also told me the name of the woman doing the same thing at the PTA meeting, and she's one of my mother's best friends." Jessica began sobbing. "Matt saw my mom's efforts to distance me from him, but I wouldn't believe him."

Josh hugged her. "It's going to be okay. As long as you love each other, nothing can separate you."

"Yes, but what else would she be capable of doing? When I called her on Sunday, she took the news of Matt's injuries very calmly." Jessica's breathing quickened.

Rachel looked at Josh with wide-open eyes while he looked down with a creased brow.

DON BRACKMAN RECEIVED a phone call as soon as he arrived at his office.

"Mr. Brackman, this is Antoni Kowalski. We've taken care of your request."

"Did you scare him?"

"Yes. Two of my men had an encounter with him while skiing on Saturday and gave him a warning."

"Okay. Good job. Let's see if *Mr. Hernandez* stops meddling in things that are none of his business."

"I'll be available if you need anything else."

JOSH CALLED PETERSON and informed him about Matt's accident. He wanted to gauge Peterson's reaction to determine whether he might know something, but his boss at the PNA showed surprise. However, as soon as Josh hung up, Peterson called Don Brackman.

"Mr. Brackman, this is Peterson."

"What do you need? We've been taking care of what you can't do."

"What? I'm just calling to let you know that Matt Hernandez is in the hospital after a serious ski accident on Saturday."

What did Kowalski do? Brackman was trying to process the information as fast as he could. "Hospitalized? Is it serious?"

"According to what his friend, Josh, told me, he went through some brain surgery and is still unconscious."

"What an unexpected event. Keep me informed."

Brackman called Antoni Kowalski. "What did you do? Can't you follow instructions?"

Kowalski was confused. "I don't understand what you're talking about."

"We talked about giving a warning to Hernandez, not sending him to the hospital."

"My men just scared him," Kowalski mumbled.

"You better control them because Hernandez is unconscious after going through brain surgery."

"But that's impossible. I trust these two guys, and they assured me that they didn't hurt Hernandez at all."

"Well, I wanted to have him scared but not involved in an accident. Suppose someone is not convinced it was an accident. In that case, we may become suspects, given his constant criticism against my company. Do you understand what you've done?" he screamed.

"I'm sorry, Mr. Brackman, but I'll talk to my guys and find out details."

"*Do it.*" And he hung up. *What a bunch of useless idiots. I better call the lawyer just in case this becomes a problem,* and he called Frank Morris.

The lawyer was in his office with his son.

"Frank, we have a potential problem that may require your services."

"What is it this time, Don?"

"You know Matt Hernandez has been meddling in things he shouldn't."

"Yes, and we're trying to monitor what he's up to."

"I know, but I also told the union contact about our problem and suggested he send a couple of guys to scare him."

"That's risky if Hernandez believes you're behind it."

"It's worse than that. Hernandez is in the hospital, unconscious."

"Did your men attack him?"

"I'm waiting for confirmation on what happened exactly but wanted to alert you in case we need to defend ourselves."

"You did well in calling me but find out what the union guys have to say and call me back. I'm going to try to find information also since Matt Hernandez is in a relationship with my partner's daughter."

Tyler followed with attention to the conversation. "More troubles with Hernandez?"

"He's hospitalized after a skiing accident. Did you hear anything from Jessica?"

Tyler pressed his lips together with a slight frown while shaking his head. "Nope."

Chapter 12

ON THE NEXT day, Sheriff White called Rachel. "Ms. Avila, we did some research on the cameras and, unfortunately, none of them captured the accident. There were few people around, given that it was late in the day. With the help of the ski patrol, we could identify your friend when he arrived at the top. Two other skiers were coming out of the gondola, as well. We checked the previous two gondola trips because sometimes skiers like to stay in the summit before going down and have five other people who could have been around when Matt started his descent. We don't know whether any of them could have done anything and will need his help to identify something or someone suspicious. Is he conscious now?"

"No, Sheriff. He responded well post-surgery but is still unconscious. The doctors say he could remain like this for a couple of days. Would it help if his friend, Josh, looks at the videos? They are close and work together, so he may recognize someone."

"I think we better wait for a couple of days and see whether Matt wakes up and remembers what happened. If not, we can get his friend to check out the videos. Let me know as soon as there is any change in Mr. Hernandez's condition."

RACHEL SHARED THE update provided by the sheriff with Jessica and Josh.

"He can't do much without Matt's help since nothing is showing on the webcams about the accident."

Josh pointed his finger. "I feel this was not an accident."

Rachel tilted her head and pressed her lips. "How about if we cover the event on TV and mention there are doubts about this being an accident?"

Josh's eyes went wide open. "Do you think we could do that?"

"I can try to convince my news producer to do some coverage here at the hospital and maybe interview both of you who can tell what you think."

"I like that." Jessica grinned.

"Let me work on it and see whether we can do something for the late news today."

FRANK MORRIS WAS at home, ready to have dinner.

"Frank, look at the news," Brackman shouted over the phone.

At that moment, Channel 5 was broadcasting live from St. Michael's Hospital.

"This is Rachel Avila with Channel 5 news at six. Matt Hernandez, a young man, is fighting for his life after suffering what appeared to be a ski accident on Saturday evening. The ski patrol report indicates that he crashed into a tree, but his fiancée and friends are puzzled about how that could have happened. Ms. Dalton, how is your fiancé doing?"

"He's still unconscious but stable."

"Do you know what happened?"

"We were skiing, and Matt decided to make the last run as he usually does. He likes the late run because he can feel the mountain's peace without so many skiers around, and he takes it slow to enjoy the scenery. He's a great skier, and it doesn't make sense to have crashed into a tree when taking a leisurely ride down the slopes."

"Mr. Josh Miller, a close friend of the victim, is also with us. Mr. Miller, do you have anything to add?"

"Just to confirm what Jessica mentioned. Knowing Matt's skiing skills, I don't believe that this was an accident and filed a police report to try to get to the bottom of it."

"Do you know someone who may have wanted to hurt Mr. Hernandez or if he has any enemies?"

"He's a great guy, and we don't know whether someone may have tried to cause the accident but still believe there's something strange going on here. I want to ask anybody who was at Crystal Mountain on Saturday and remembers anything related to this incident to please contact the sheriff's office at Crystal County or us."

"Thank you to both of you." Rachel looked at the camera. *"This is Rachel Avila reporting live from St. Michael's Hospital. Goodnight."*

As soon as the cameras turned off, Rachel looked at Jessica.

"Good job. It may trigger some reaction from someone involved in Matt's accident or who may have witnessed something. We'll wait and see if something comes up."

"Thank you, Rachel." Jessica hugged her.

Don Brackman called Frank again. "Did you see? They are already insinuating that it's not an accident."

"Have you checked on what your guys did?"

"Yes, and they said they didn't touch Matt Hernandez. Just ran downhill close to him and gave him a verbal warning."

"Are you sure that's what they did?"

"I'm fairly sure they wouldn't lie to me. What do we do now?"

"Nothing. First, the police must prove it wasn't an accident, and then, if there was foul play, they will need to figure out who was involved. I don't think you need to worry about it, but just in case, my advice is to tell those two guys who were part of the warning to disappear."

"Will do. You mentioned having some contacts in the press. Can you use them to avoid this type of news?"

"Yes, and I already alerted my contacts but remember that we talked before about avoiding a campaign against DB Corp. This incident is different, but I'll recheck with them to make sure it doesn't grow out of control."

THE DALTONS ALSO watched the news and were surprised to see their daughter on camera.

Mary shook her head. "I don't know why Jessica is saying those things."

"Maybe because she believes that someone is behind it." John stared at his wife.

"Are you suggesting that I had something to do with it?"

He had a twisted half-smile on his face. "You're saying it, not me."

"Oh, for God's sake. How could you believe that I would try to hurt Matt? I have to admit that

135

I don't think he's the right person for our daughter but going from there to think that I could do such a thing is preposterous." Mary's eyes were on fire, and she left the room.

John snorted while staring into space and then got on the phone. "Jessica, this is Dad."

"Are you going to judge me for being on the news?"

"Not at all. First, how is Matt doing?"

"The same. Still unconscious."

"I hope he wakes up soon. I just wanted to ask who you think may want to hurt him."

"Not sure, Dad. You know he's been actively working with the PNA and investigating DB Corp. He and Josh talked to someone who warned them that they could get in trouble if they didn't stop."

"For investigating the wastewater compliance issue? That seems to be an exaggeration. Why would a large corporation try to hurt a person for asking questions?"

"I don't know, but when Josh talked to the Crystal County Sheriff and mentioned DB Corp., he showed some interest based on his personal experience from fifteen years ago when there was a big fire at the brewery. The sheriff was part of the team investigating the event and was not on board with how the case was closed in a few days. He believes that DB Corp. used undue influences in their favor to stop the police from looking into it further."

"Wow. You know we've been providing legal services to DB Corp. for many years and don't see any irregularities. They are trying to make money and sometimes use contacts to improve their position, but that's not unusual for large corporations. Because of their size, they have access to high-level authorities, but it doesn't mean they are acting illegally."

"There's something more, Dad."

"What is it?"

"Did you know that mom has been trying to get Matt's promotion denied?"

John slumped into a chair. *Mary, what have you done?* He took a few seconds to respond. "I know your mom doesn't think Matt is the right person for you."

She interrupted, "And that's why she went to talk to the principal at Lakeview and then sent her close friends to repeat the criticism for Matt's promotion at the PTA meeting?"

He closed his eyes and mumbled. "I didn't know those things."

"Okay, Dad. I don't want to argue with you now. Maybe you can find out more about the role of the firm at the time of that big fire at the brewery?"

"I wasn't at the firm then, but if it interests you, I'll ask a few questions. DB Corp. was already one of Frank's clients, and he brought them into our portfolio when we became partners."

"Thanks, Dad. I have to go. I just saw the doctor

in the hallway and want to talk to him." She hung up and walked toward the doctor. "Dr. Becker, any news?" Jessica repeatedly swallowed while looking at the doctor."

"We ran a new scan, and it's reporting some new activity in his brain, so we're confident that he may wake up soon. If he does, we'll move him to a regular room."

"Oh, thank you, Dr. Becker." Jessica's eyes brightened.

Chapter 13

J OHN DALTON WALKED into his partner's office the next day. "Good morning, Frank. Do you have a couple of minutes?"

"Of course," he said with a big smile on his face, "how's Matt doing?"

"He's doing better and may wake up any moment, according to the physicians. Did you see my daughter's interview on TV last night?"

"Yes. I can't figure out why Jessica suspects it wasn't an accident. Mr. Brackman called me worried about the implications that someone may have tried to hurt Matt. He's afraid that DB Corp. may be dragged into the story if the quest for wastewater compliance that Matt and the PNA have against the brewery is known."

John stared at Frank. "Why would he worry if there's nothing to hide?"

"Don't tell me that you believe that conspiracy theory." He waved his hand in dismissal. "It wouldn't surprise me to find out that this may be part of the campaign to discredit DB Corp."

John tilted his head and kept intense eye contact. "Are you saying that my daughter could be part of a campaign against the brewery? C'mon, we both know Jessica, and she wouldn't do it. I talked to her, and she believes what Matt told her about the warnings he received for investigating too much."

"Nonsense."

"Let me ask you something else. Were you involved in providing legal advice to DB Corp. when there was a fire at the brewery several years ago?"

"Yes. That was more than fifteen years ago, and I had the opportunity to work with the corporation and get them exonerated from any wrongdoing. The authorities ruled the case an accident due to a short circuit and declared the company free of liability. They made substantial donations to the workers' families who lost their lives and then rebuilt the facilities. Mr. Brackman recognized my contributions by retaining me as his lawyer, and then you know I brought the account to our firm. Why do you ask?"

"Some people are not convinced of the investigation's thoroughness and wonder whether high-level influences were used to close the case quickly and without any impact on DB Corp."

Frank flinched. "I don't know what they're talking about. The investigation was fast and efficient. Who are those people?"

"It doesn't matter. I was just curious about the story surrounding our largest client."

"We still may have the folders around if you or someone needs information about the resolution of that incident."

"Don't worry. As I said, I was just intrigued about how the relationship with the client started. I won't take up any more of your time." *I'm sure there is nothing in those folders, but his demeanor is suspicious.* John stood and left the office.

JESSICA AND JOSH were chatting in the waiting room when Dr. Becker walked toward them with firm strides and a smile. "He's conscious and in ten minutes will be moved to a regular room. From now on, you can see him during normal hours visiting hours."

Jessica hugged him. "Wonderful. Thank you for all you've done."

And Josh pumped his fist up in the air. "*Yeah.*"

"I'm happy for him and for both of you who have been here all the time but let me warn you that he may not remember some things."

Jessica's lip quivered. "What?"

"Don't worry. It's quite common to temporarily lose memory in these cases, especially those surrounding the event that caused the injury. It's called post-traumatic amnesia and may last a few hours, weeks, or months, but patients recover the memory over time in general. In the beginning, he may have problems remembering short-term things such as appointments, where he left his keys, or to pass along a phone message, but that's not always the case."

"How about remembering the incident? The police would like to talk to him." Josh held his breath.

"That's the most difficult part. The brain usually removes those moments, but with the help of people who have some information about the accident like you, first responders, and physicians, he may be able to reconstruct what took place."

Matt looked and seemed somewhat confused when they entered the room, but then a grin illuminated his face, and he mumbled, "Jessica, Josh."

She ran toward his side and gave him a soft and long kiss. "We've been waiting for you to wake up."

"What am I doing here?" Matt shrugged.

"You had an accident on the slopes Saturday and have been unconscious until now."

"And what day is today?"

"Wednesday." Josh approached the bed from the other side and smiled at his friend. "Do you remember going skiing together?"

His eyes were darting. "Not really."

"It's okay," Jessica took his hand, "the doctor said you may not remember some things initially but will recover your memory soon. You just need to relax now, and we'll help you."

"I remember driving with Josh to Crystal Mountain, but then everything is blurred in my head."

"That's a good start. We'll go through what you did the rest of the day but not now." Jessica's smiled, trying to look upbeat.

"Do you remember your job?" Josh kept steady eye contact.

Matt looked into space. "A teacher? *I'm a teacher,*" he shouted and turned to Josh, "and you're my partner at the PNA."

"Wonderful, my friend. Welcome back." Josh rubbed his hands together. "Our team is back."

"Okay, okay, that's enough, you two. Don't start talking about work or the PNA now." Jessica shook with laughter.

They kept chatting for about an hour until a nurse came to check on the patient and recommended letting him rest. Jessica and Josh left the room, walking with energy and enthusiastically talking as if the exhaustion and fears of the last few days had magically disappeared.

"I'm going to my parent's house to take a warm shower and sleep a little. I know when this adrenaline is gone, I will drop into bed like a log."

"Go," Josh smiled, "you deserve some rest. We'll

need some energy to help Matt in the next few days. I'll tell Rachel the news. She's going to be happy."

WHEN JESSICA GOT to her parent's house, Mary was in the living room, glancing over some magazines. She got up when seeing her daughter. "Hi, Jessica. Everything okay with Matt?"

"Yes. He's conscious now but may take some time to get back his memory."

"I'm glad he's recovering." Jessica looked at her without saying a word. "Your father will arrive soon. Are you staying for dinner?"

"Yes." And she turned around and went upstairs to her room.

Dinner was served an hour later. Nobody said much while eating the delicious pork chops in wine sauce prepared by the chef until John broke the tense silence.

"Jessica, tell us more about Matt's condition."

She explained what the doctors had said, and Mary asked about his recollection of the incident.

"How about the accident. Did he describe what happened?"

"No, Mom. Are you worried about what he could remember?" Jessica gazed at her.

Mary fidgeted. "Why should I be?"

"Because we think Matt wasn't hurt in an *accident*. We believe someone was involved in making him lose control and crash against the tree."

Mary's eyes went wide open. "*What?* Who might have wanted to hurt him?"

"We don't know yet, but I know that you don't like him." Jessica narrowed her eyes.

"Why do you say that? He's been into this home, and we've treated him well."

"Yes, but you also tried to block his promotion."

Mary put her hands over her open mouth.

"Don't deny it. Mrs. Douglas told me about your conversation during the school board meeting and then your friend, Amy's, comments at the PTA. How could you go so far? And involving your friends? That's despicable." Jessica paused and, keeping her gaze on her mother, added, "Did you have anything to do with Matt's accident?"

"How could you?" Mary started sobbing.

"Okay." John tried to lower the tension. "Jessica, you've been under a lot of stress and are tired, so maybe this isn't the time to talk about this. Your mother did something wrong because she's been looking out for what she believes is best for you. Accusing her of causing Matt's accident is leaping to inappropriate conclusions for the time being. Why don't we relax a little and enjoy a nice dessert before going to bed? Tomorrow everything is going to look different."

Jessica threw her napkin onto the table, got up, and went into her room.

John looked at his wife. "You didn't answer the question."

Mary's glaring eyes and flushed face turned to her husband. "Neither of you *believes* me." Then she left the room with firm steps.

JESSICA ENTERED MATT's room at the hospital and saw him sitting on the bed and having breakfast. "It looks like you've built up some appetite."

He smiled while swallowing a muffin. "I'm so hungry that even this hospital food tastes amazing."

"That's a good sign. Did you sleep well and remember new things?"

"I've had a good night's sleep, maybe helped by the drugs they gave me, and feel good. I remember things from my childhood, my parents, and my job at the school, but still running blank on how the accident happened."

"Don't worry about it. The doctor said it would take some time to figure it out, but you're doing well. Have you talked to Dr. Becker?"

"Yes, and he said I'm making good progress."

"Aww, I'm so proud of you," she said and kissed him on the lips.

"Wow, with this type of medicine, I'm going to

be out of here any time now. The doctor told me you'd been around all the time while I was unconscious. I love you," he said and then kissed her hand.

"Hey, are we interrupting a romantic moment?" Josh and Rachel walked into the room.

"Yes, but I forgive you since you've also been here and supporting Jess over the last few days."

"Okay, man, let's not get all smooshy here." Josh gave him a high five. "I see you're doing well, and there are a lot of things to catch up on."

Matt rubbed his hands together. "I'm ready. Bring it on."

"Okay, Mr. Hernandez," Jessica's tone didn't give room for discussions, "it's great to see you with a lot of energy, but you've got to pace your recovery."

"Jessica's right, partner. We can chat a little about things that have gone on in the last few weeks to see whether you can recall what we were doing, but let's not jump ahead. We need to focus on the day of the accident to try to reconstruct what happened."

"I've been trying to," Matt shook his head, "but I can't go beyond us being together at the café and then my going to the gondola. After that, everything is blank."

"At least you remember being there that day. That's good progress, Matt. Maybe when the doctor discharges you, we can go to Crystal Mountain and see whether being there helps."

"That's a good idea, Jessica. And we can schedule

a visit with Sheriff White. He has some videos of people who were around at the same time you were at the summit. It may trigger something in your mind," Rachel added.

Chapter 14

FRANK MORRIS WENT to the DB Corp. building to talk to his client. Don Brackman saw him outside his office and waved him to come in. The two men shook hands and had a light chat over coffee until Don put down his cup and reclined back in his chair with his fingers intertwined.

"What is the latest on Matt Hernandez? Did you hear anything from your partner and his daughter?"

"Yes. He's recovering but doesn't remember anything about the incident."

"That's good news. Would that be permanent?"

"Nobody knows, but the doctors say sometimes the memory loss is temporary."

Don adjusted his cuffs. "I hope that's not the case."

"We need to plan for all possible scenarios. What if he remembers that two men tried to intimidate him?"

"Those men are far away right now and won't come back for a long time."

"Matt may recognize them if there are videos. If that were the case, could they be traced back to you?"

"I doubt it," Brackman looked up, "but that's a good question. I'm going to make sure there is no link to DB Corp."

"Okay. Remember that our partners don't want to attract any attention to the company's operations."

"I know. We'll keep a low profile in running the brewery."

"By the way, our partners are not happy about the way you're handling the wastewater issue. They understand that you're trying to save some money by delaying the investment in water-treating equipment, but if it brings focus to the brewery, they suggest that you don't postpone it any longer. You know the benefits from having the brewery running smoothly more than compensate for that investment."

Brackman crossed his arms. "I've been running this operation for many years, and we've *all* benefited from it." He looked Frank straight into the eyes. "Tell our *partners* that I don't need suggestions on how to do it."

Frank knew the volatile temperament of Brackman, so he inhaled and extended the palms of his hands, making a slight movement downward. "Nobody is trying to tell you how to run the business. We just think that lately, the PNA seems to be getting out of control, and we have those couple of individuals asking questions and sniffing around. We know they've been in contact with the fishermen. If this grows and the media gets involved, our contacts will no longer protect us. Just imagine the stories that some creative reporter could put together around Matt Hernandez's accident, who has been vocally attacking DB Corp. And by the way, a Channel 5 reporter has been in contact with him."

Brackman's eyes went wide open.

"Making that investment now may help to appease the concerns of those groups and avoid further investigations."

"I see your point," Brackman's fingers tapped on his desk, "let me think about it."

Dr. Becker did the afternoon routine check on Matt's condition. "How do you feel, Matt?"

"I feel great, no pain, can maintain conversations with my friends, and remember things, except for the accident."

"Don't worry. That's normal. It may take some more time. In some cases, patients go back to a normal life, but others lose the details of the incident that caused the concussion. You've had a good recovery, and I'll sign your discharge for tomorrow so you can spend the weekend with family and friends."

"*Yay*," Jessica clapped her hands. "Can he do normal activities?"

"Yes, you can," the physician looked at Matt, "but remember that you had a concussion and surgery five days ago, so don't go crazy."

"I promise, Dr. Becker, he'll behave." Jessica grinned.

"It looks like you're in good hands, Matt." The doctor winked at him.

When the doctor left the room, Josh approached him. "Is there anything we should do or look for with Matt?"

"Just monitor how he behaves and be patient. He still may not remember what he does or says, especially in the short term. For example, last night, after having dinner, he asked when dinner would be served. The nurse went through what he ate, and then he remembered. Incidents like that may happen during the next couple of weeks, but it's okay."

THE MEMBERS OF the law firm of Morris, Dalton, and Associates received the news of Matt's release with mixed emotions. John walked into Frank's office, where he was reviewing some documents with Tyler.

"Got a call from Jessica, and Matt is going to be released from the hospital tomorrow."

Frank raised his eyebrows. "Is that so? So soon?"

Tyler looked down while running his hand through his hair without saying a word.

John shook his head. "It looks like you two are not excited about this." Then he left the room.

Frank called Don Brackman to share what he heard. "Matt Hernandez is getting out of the hospital tomorrow. We need to monitor what he's doing but don't make another stupid move."

"Understood. I've been thinking about what you said this morning and decided to go ahead and approve the investment in the equipment needed to comply with the wastewater regulations. We're not in our strongest financial position now but need to reduce the attention on our operations."

"Good to hear that, Don. It's a wise decision. Hernandez and his friends won't have any reason to keep sniffing around. Maybe they'll also forget to keep investigating the cause of his accident."

"Hope so. Our PR department is drafting an announcement related to the investment that will be sent to you for review."

"Great. We'll look at it and provide our comments. The sooner we get this out to the public, the better."

JESSICA AND JOSH went to pick up Matt at the hospital. When they entered the room, he was reading and smiled when he noticed their presence.

"Hi, Matt, are you ready?" Jessica's eyes sparkled.

Matt tilted his head. "Ready for what?"

Josh looked at Jessica. "Dr. Becker discharged you, and we're here to take you home."

"Ahh," Matt smacked his palm against his forehead, "yes, of course," and he began getting out of bed. "Let's get out of this place."

Matt lived in a two-bedroom condo situated across from a park. The living room had a sliding door leading to a balcony that Jessica opened to bring in some fresh air. The simple furniture and thrifty decoration were expected from a bachelor's place, but the whole apartment was spotless, showing the owner's meticulous personality. After a few minutes, Rachel joined them to plan what to do in the next couple of days.

"Good to be home." Matt threw his hand up into the air.

Jessica hugged him. "We're all happy you're here."

"Yep. That was quite an accident you had just a week ago." Josh nodded and stretched his arms.

"Okay. It's been a rough week, but now it's time to celebrate." Rachel produced a bottle of merlot, and they all cheered.

They chatted on the balcony for a while until

Matt went inside, sat on a brown fabric sofa, and invited them to take a seat around a small coffee table.

"Let's review where we were before the accident happened."

"The water sample we took near the brewery showed levels of contamination around four times what is allowed by the regulations," Josh shared with a furrowed brow.

"I know that an isolated sample is not a valid measurement for the law, but would it be enough to capture the interest of your channel for the story?" Matt looked at Rachel.

"Maybe, but I want to share what I found. Remember you told me to review old files for coverage of the big fire at the brewery fifteen years ago?"

"Big fire?" Matt's eyes were wide open.

Rachel froze for a second, and Josh jumped in. "Remember we went to visit Mario Ramirez, the operator who retired from the brewery, and he told us about the fire that nobody seemed to investigate in-depth?"

"Oh, sorry, my memory is trying to catch up. Rachel, please continue. Did you find anything?"

"I think so. Looking at the news from that time, I found something intriguing about a witness at the scene of the fire." Now all eyes were on Rachel. "When the Channel 5 crew arrived, one operator described the accident as beginning at the lab and producing a series of explosions that created embers shooting off the fire and expanding into the warehouse. He said everything happened quickly, and there was a smell like benzene or solvents used for paints. However, that witness changed his story, and those original comments were never included in the incident report or investigated."

"I remember that guy, Mario Ramirez." Matt nodded, but Josh grinned and didn't let him continue.

"Good memory, Matt, *impressive*."

"Thanks. You see. I'll remember all the bad things you've done to me also." Matt pointed his finger at his friend with a smile. "As I was saying before this smart guy interrupted me, Mario also told us that the company closely protected access to the site."

Rachel leaned forward. "And that's the same thing Sheriff White mentioned. He was a young officer then, and he and others were surprised by the case's fast-closing. We need to pay a visit to the sheriff to talk about that. He also has some videos of the day of your accident."

"Let's go tomorrow," Matt exclaimed.

"Wait a minute." Jessica had been quiet. "Remember that you have to go slowly and not stress yourself out. Besides, tomorrow is Sunday, and there will be a bunch of people on the mountain. If we want to talk to the sheriff and see the videos, we better wait until the weekend crowd is gone. That way, we can take a trip on the gondola to the summit and see whether that helps Matt remember what happened that day."

Matt took Jessica's hand and looked at Josh. "You see why I'm going to marry this woman? She's smart, takes care of me, and she's beautiful."

They all laughed and agreed that Rachel would try to contact the sheriff, and all of them would take it easy on Sunday by going to a famous café near a park downtown for brunch and then follow that with a movie.

Chapter 15

ON MONDAY, THE newspapers covered the local brewery's announcement related to its wastewater treatment equipment.

THE PRESIDENT OF DB CORP., MR. DON BRACKMAN ANNOUNCED AN INVESTMENT OF THREE MILLION DOLLARS IN WASTEWATER FACILITIES THAT SHOWS THE COMPANY'S COMMITMENT TO THE COMMUNITY AND ITS ADHERENCE TO THE STRICTEST PRACTICES TO PROTECT THE ENVIRONMENT. BRACKMAN EMPHASIZED THAT SOCIAL RESPONSIBILITY HAS BEEN A CORE VALUE THAT HAS GUIDED DB CORP. MANAGEMENT SINCE ITS FOUNDING EIGHTY YEARS AGO.

THE PRESIDENT OF THE PNA, MR. PETERSON, PRAISED THE DECISION.

HE SAID IT'S ANOTHER EXAMPLE OF CORPORATE AND COMMUNITY PARTNERSHIP IN SECURING A SAFE ENVIRONMENT FOR OUR FUTURE GENERATIONS.

"Did you read the paper this morning?" Josh waved the newspaper while coming into Matt's apartment as soon as he opened the door.

"What? What is so important that got you so excited?"

He handed him the paper. "Look at it yourself."

Matt began reading and then froze while staring with wide eyes. Jessica was reading over his shoulder and grinned. "But this is good. You got what you wanted."

"Yes, but somehow I smell a rat." Matt threw the paper and began pacing the room while Josh sat in a chair, looking down.

"Why do you say that?" Jessica couldn't understand why they were so upset.

"Honey," Matt stood in front of her, "Josh and I met at DB Corp. offices with their PR manager. She did not mention anything about it and made a point that the brewery followed wastewater regulations and filed for an extension of the grace period."

"Yes, and that was ten days ago." Josh supported his friend's argument. "Why would they confront the PNA if they were planning to invest? And the announcement doesn't say anything about delays in equipment delivery. Why wait until now to announce it if they decided to invest some time ago and ordered the equipment? Why not address that issue as well?"

"I see your point now." Jessica twisted her mouth and shook her head. "My father also mentioned that the bankruptcy of the supplier delayed the delivery of the equipment. I'll talk to him to get his thoughts."

"That's a good idea, Jessica. See if he can help us understand why they made this announcement now and what changed their minds."

JESSICA WENT TO the offices of Morris, Dalton, and Associates and found her father immersed in preparing for a case. She smiled from the half-opened door. "May I come in?"

"Of course, honey. How is Matt doing?"

"Better, thank you. He's in full control of his mind except for some brief moments where he needs help to remember things. But it's within the normal course of recovery from his concussion. He's thinking about going back to work next week."

"That's remarkable." He nodded. "I'm sure that your being by his side is helping a lot." Then he winked.

"It's been quite a challenge," she sighed, "but we're both happy that it's almost over." She sat across from her father and leaned on the desk. "I have a question for you."

"Shoot. What do you need from me?"

"We saw the announcement made by DB Corp. this morning related to their investment in water-treatment facilities, and it looked rather strange that they suddenly made that move after prolonging it for over a year. Do you know anything about their decision?"

John moved back in his chair and clenched his hands. "I'm also intrigued by it and will get together with Frank in thirty minutes to ask him since he's managing that account. Feel free to join if you'd like."

"I'd love to. Matt and Josh are suspicious and find it hard to believe that DB Corp. has changed its position so drastically overnight."

"I understand. Let's see what Frank has to say." John looked his daughter in the eyes. "Can I ask you something also?"

Her eyes went wide. "Of course."

"We haven't seen you in a while because you were spending time at the hospital and now at Matt's apartment. Would you mind coming home and talking with your mother? The last time we were together, the conversation turned rather contemptuous, and I believe you need to rebuild the relationship you have with your mom. I know she's done some things against Matt that can't be justified, but she loves you and, in her own way, is trying to do what's best for you. Maybe having another chat now would help. I can't take this situation where you're not talking to each other. Could you do that?"

She looked down. "I know I was harsh with Mom, but I was stressed thinking someone was behind Matt's accident. We still don't believe it was an accident, but I'll talk to her."

"I appreciate it. You can come with Matt and have dinner with us if that's okay with both of you."

"Thanks, Dad. I'll talk to him and let you know. I don't want to interrupt you anymore. See you in a few minutes in Frank's office."

"HELLO, JESSICA. GOOD to see you back. How's Matt?" Frank stood up and invited Jessica and John to sit around a small table surrounded by four maroon leather chairs in his office.

Jessica sat across from her father. "He's doing better and enjoying being out of the hospital. Thank you for asking. Is Tyler going to join us?"

"No. He's out of town for a week or longer. John, you asked to see me this morning. What can I do for you?" Frank turned to his partner.

"It's about the DB Corp. announcement. Since you're the main contact with Don Brackman, I thought you might know more about why they decided to go public with the announcement of the investment in wastewater control equipment."

"They just thought that it would be a good PR move." Frank shrugged.

John leaned on the table. "But they have been trying to avoid that investment, and suddenly the company moves ahead with it. Isn't it a little strange?"

"Corporations make decisions all the time based on particular strategic or financial considerations, so they might have reviewed the situation and decided to move. I don't have an answer, and while seeing a change in direction, I wouldn't say that it bothers me," and turning to Jessica, he said, "Matt and the PNA must be happy now."

"They are because the wastewater problem is going to be solved, but still, we're wondering about the timing."

Frank thought for a few seconds and responded with a tight-lipped smile. "I don't know what the PNA wants. First, they complained about the lack of response from DB Corp. to the environmental regulations. Now, they are suspicious about the timing of the investment announcement that will address the problem they spotlighted. I believe they should enjoy their victory and move on, leaving DB Corp. to run their business. They are our best client and, as far as I know, we will support them on whatever legal matter they need."

"Understood, Frank," John stared at him, "one more question. Do you know whether the equipment they claim they had ordered from Italy will finally be coming?"

Frank sighed. "I don't know whether they are proceeding with that vendor or a different one, but it's not our responsibility to ask those questions."

"Certainly not, but we may need to file a revision of the application since we based it on the delays in receiving the equipment due to the bankruptcy of the manufacturer."

"We may," Frank checked his watch, "but I wouldn't worry about it for now."

"Okay, thanks for the update. Let me know whether there is anything I have to do." John stood up and left his partner's office, followed by Jessica.

"Dad, do you think he told us all he knows?" Jessica asked her father when they went back to John's office.

"Not sure but based on the close relationship he has with Don Brackman, I doubt that he would be so calm unless he knew more. I assume that Matt and Josh would stop their quest against DB Corp. now, right?"

"It depends. We still want to have answers to the cause of Matt's accident. If DB Corp. had anything to do with it, Matt and Josh will keep going to understand why Matt was targeted. They also have questions related to the brewery fire."

"What about it?"

"You know they talked to an ex-employee of the brewery, who is suspicious about how quickly the investigation was closed. Sheriff White from Crystal County, who is looking into Matt's accident, mentioned to Rachel Avila that he was part of that investigation as a young officer and was also shocked to see that leads were not followed. In Channel 5's old files, Rachel also found that witnesses mentioned a series of explosions during the fire that could indicate some flammable material was present. Still, the final report of the accident ignored all of that. DB Corp. seems to hide other things beyond the wastewater issue."

John puffed his cheeks and exhaled. "I think you're right. Something isn't clear about this client. I asked Frank about his relationship with DB Corp., as you suggested. He gave me some generalities on how his handling of the fire case earned Don Brackman's trust and a large retainer to handle all DB Corp.'s legal matters. It must have saved the company a lot of money. Let me know if you find anything else and whether I could be of any help."

"Thanks, Dad. Matt and Josh will be happy to know that."

"Great. Remember that you're coming home with Matt for dinner tonight."

MATT RECEIVED THE news of the invitation to have dinner at the Dalton's house with a frown.

Jessica took his hands and looked into his eyes. "I know you're hurt by what my mom did to you, but Dad says she's sorry about it. I also had a conversation with him at the office, and he's beginning to be suspicious about Frank's relationship with DB Corp., so he may be able to help us if we want to investigate them."

That got Matt's attention. "Okay, if you think it's good to see your family, I'll go, but please understand that I still don't trust your mother."

"I don't blame you, but let's hear what she has to say. Remember that you pick your friends but not your family, and that's what we got." Her bright smile didn't provide room for any objection.

JESSICA PARKED HER BMW in the Dalton's driveway, and the maid opened the door when they rang the bell. "Good evening, Ms. Jessica; your parents are waiting for you on the patio. Good to see you again, Mr. Hernandez."

They went across the lavishly decorated living room onto the terrace through a double-panel sliding door. The Daltons had placed a dining table set up for four next to the terrace's railing with a magnificent view of the sunset over the river.

"Hello." John stepped forward, hugged his daughter, and extended his hand to Matt. "I'm happy to see you've recovered from the accident. Are you feeling well?"

"Thank you, John. I can say that I feel much

better than I did a week ago." Matt shook his hand and smiled.

"Mary is coming in a minute. We thought it would be nice to have dinner outdoors if you don't mind. The weather is cool, but the heater will keep us warm, and I'm sure you'll enjoy the view."

The house was built on a small hill overlooking the river's mouth and the bay, with the town's skyscrapers showing their silhouette with a few lights on. A red glow over the horizon created a path of light broken by a sailboat coming back to the harbor's safe. The three of them were enjoying that peaceful moment when a voice from behind interrupted them.

"Hello, Jessica, Matt." Mary came through the sliding doors wearing a green palazzo jumpsuit enhanced by a gold necklace. "Glad you could come tonight. Matt, you look great. How are you doing?"

Matt briefly glanced at his fiancée. "I'm doing well. Thanks for asking."

Mary looked down and away. "Matt, I don't know how to say this, but I'm sorry about the confusion on your promotion."

"Confusion?" Jessica stared at her mother.

"Yes, it was a huge misunderstanding. I just asked Mrs. Williams about Matt's credentials since I was surprised by the decision to promote someone so young. As a Lakeview board member, I feel responsible for ensuring the highest proficiency level and just wanted to check the decision basis. It was more a question on Mrs. Williams's decision-making process than criticism to Matt." She looked at him. "I didn't have any intention to challenge your capabilities, but it looks like there was a misinterpretation of my inquiry, and I feel bad about it."

"And how about your friend, Amy, also questioning Matt's promotion at the PTA." Jessica wasn't convinced of her mother's sincerity.

"I made a comment to my friends about my thoughts on Mrs. Williams's decision to promote Matt, and they took it on their own to further challenge the principal's choice."

"Okay," John interrupted, "I think we've talked enough about this *misunderstanding*. We're here to celebrate that Matt has recovered, so why don't we sit at the table and enjoy a nice dinner. Wouldn't you agree, Matt?"

Matt grinned. "Of course, John. Good food always cheers me up," and looking at Mary, "and don't worry, Mary, all that is in the past, and you don't need to feel bad about it."

They relished an apple-butternut squash soup followed by a caramelized chicken with lemon and green onions and then moved inside for coffee and dessert.

While savoring the strawberries, John looked at Matt. "What are your plans now?"

"If the recovery continues, I think I'm going to return to work next week. I'm feeling well and don't have any memory problems, except for the moment before the accident."

Jessica put down her coffee. "And we're going to go tomorrow to Crystal Mountain to see whether that helps him to remember the incident."

Mary moved nervously in her chair. "And why do you need to do it? Couldn't the stress of reviving the environment surrounding the accident be counterproductive to Matt's full recovery? What is important is that he's recovering well, so why risk a fallback?"

"Mom," Jessica sighed, "we don't think it was an accident, and if that's true, we need to find out who was behind it because it may happen again."

"That's fine." John nodded. "I don't think that going to the mountain could hurt his recovery."

"But skiing could be dangerous while still recovering," Mary tried once more.

"We're not going skiing. We'll ride the gondola to the top to see whether that triggers some memories and meet with Sheriff White, who's going to show us some videos taken that day by the mountain's cameras."

John offered to help with any legal action that might be required if it were proven that Matt's injuries were not produced by an accident but by some aggression or irresponsible behavior.

When leaving the Daltons' residence, Jessica turned to Matt. "Did you believe what my mother said about the misinterpretation of her chat with Mrs. Williams?"

Matt shrugged. "Not sure, but it could be possible. Anyway, we can give her the benefit of the doubt."

"And did you see how she got uncomfortable when we talked about going to Crystal Mountain tomorrow to investigate the cause of your accident?"

He shook his head. "Are you getting a little paranoid about your mother? Last week you were offended when I suggested that she might have been involved in challenging my promotion, and now, you're overreacting and creating a conspiracy theory. I look at it from the point of view that they invited us for dinner, and she provided some explanation and all that is positive."

"Maybe you're right. She takes her role as a Lakeview board member very seriously and feels accountable for it. Let's assume that's the case."

Chapter 16

EARLY IN THE morning, Jessica, Matt, Josh, and Rachel got into Jessica's car and made the two-hour drive to Crystal Mountain. It was a clear morning with some clouds, and the opportunity to take a break and go to the mountains kept everybody in a good mood. They left the car at the parking lot at the mountain's base and walked toward the gondola station, happy to wear everyday footwear and not heavy ski boots. There was a short line of excited skiers ready to live the day's adventures and eager to demonstrate their skills on the mountain. While riding to the summit with four skiers, Matt quietly observed the slopes extending below like white fingers among the snow-spotted pines.

Jessica noticed his behavior. "Are you okay?"

"Yes, just looking and trying to remember the last time I rode this gondola."

"Any memories?"

"It vaguely comes to mind that the snow was brighter, and there weren't as many people."

"That's good, Matt." Josh nodded. "It was a beautiful afternoon, and the last ride of the day, there are usually not many people."

"Yes, I remember. I was sitting, looking forward, and two guys were sitting across from me, chatting."

"Good." Jessica smiled. "Maybe you can remember other things at the top."

The twelve-minute ride seemed to recharge Matt's brain. When they got to the top, the other skiers adjusted their goggles. They began their descent among laughter and challenges to make it in the fastest time.

Matt and his friends stood near the summit station, looking around for clues that would bring back memories.

"I remember getting out of the gondola and spending a few minutes enjoying the scenery."

"How about those guys who rode the gondola with you?" Josh stared at him. "Do you remember seeing them going down the slope?"

Matt looked far away for a moment and shook his head. "I don't remember seeing those guys going down."

"Did you notice whether they stayed around?"

Matt's eyes went wide. "I think I do. They were just chatting while fixing their equipment before I decided to begin my descent."

Jessica tilted her head with a furrowed brow. "What does that tell us?"

"It may mean those guys had something to do with Matt's accident. If someone tried to attack him, they would have come from behind." Josh pointed up.

"As soon as I can ski again, I'll go to see the site of the accident. That may help also," Matt replied.

"I think looking at the videos, we may be able to confirm if the guys left the summit after Matt. There's a camera at the exit of this gondola station." Rachel moved her head in that direction.

After a few more minutes, it was time to meet Sheriff White, who was expecting them at his office.

"Good morning, Sheriff. Thank you for seeing us." Rachel extended her hand and introduced the others.

"Glad you're here. Hopefully, we'll see whether we can help. We have reviewed the videos from the different cameras, but none of them captured the moment of the accident. Maybe when Matt sees them, he'll remember something. Let's go to the conference room where we have the screen."

The conference room didn't have any windows, and the only pieces of furniture were a table and six chairs. A screen on one end and a projector on the other completed the simple layout. They sat around, looking at different videos captured by the various cameras until they got to the one that recorded the scene at the top gondola station.

"There you are, Matt." Josh pointed to the screen.

"I see, and those were the two guys who rode in the gondola with me. I remember them wearing identical green beanies. It looks like they were having fun, chatting before heading down."

Josh looked at the sheriff. "Or that they were waiting for you to go first?"

"Wait," Rachel interrupted, "there is another guy with a snowboard. He didn't ride with you on the gondola, so he may have been at the summit before you got there."

"And he began the descent after the other two skiers went down," the sheriff showed him on the screen.

"I think I recognize that blue parka." Jessica's eyes went wide open. "Can we rewind and freeze the image?"

The sheriff did, and she shouted, "That looks like *Tyler*."

"You're right, Jessica. Tyler was wearing a blue parka that day, and even if the goggles cover his face, that seems to be him." Josh raised his eyebrows.

"A snowboard?" Matt mumbled.

"Let's see if we can identify when he got to the summit." The sheriff scrolled down to a previous video. "There he is. He got to the summit in the gondola trip before yours. Do you know the guy?"

Josh tilted his head. "Why would he wait at the top?"

"There are bathrooms at the summit. He may have used the facilities."

Jessica's eyes narrowed. "Or he might have waited for Matt."

"What reason would he have to wait for Matt?" the sheriff asked.

"Earlier in the day, he had tried to convince me that Matt was cheating on me with another woman. When Matt arrived, there was an argument and Matt punched him. Then he left, making threats."

Matt was immersed in his thoughts and suddenly shouted, "I remember now. Those guys with the green beanies got in my way and positioned themselves in front and on one side, leaving no room to go except to follow them. They guided me to the black slope."

"Did they push you to the side?" Jessica held her breath.

"No." Matt shook his head while looking down. "After going down a few hundred yards, they moved away and shouted something like *this is a warning*."

"Maybe the shock caused by the situation made you lose control and hit the tree?" Sheriff White leaned on the table.

"No. There was something else." Matt stared at the ceiling like he was searching for an answer and then gazed at the sheriff. "The *snowboarder*. Someone on a snowboard skidded close to me, sending a flurry of snow that made me lose control." Matt tilted his head back and yelled, "That's what happened."

"Did you recognize Tyler?" Jessica put her hands over her mouth.

"No, everything went too fast, and I was in shock after those two guys bullied me, so I only remember that it was someone on a snowboard."

"Okay," Sheriff White scratched his head, "we have a couple of hypotheses. Two guys rode in the gondola and waited for you to go down to follow you and deliver some sort of threat. Then we have another guy who you know and who argued with you. He waited at the summit and made an unsafe move on his snowboard that caused you to lose control. Do we think that the three of them could have acted in coordination?"

Rachel opened her hands. "It's possible, but why shout that it was a warning if they intended to hurt Matt?"

"Maybe they didn't calculate that Matt could lose control and crash?" Josh looked to the screen with his arms crossed.

"I think there are two possible reasons to try to hurt me. One could be a warning to stop me from continuing the investigation on DB Corp., and the second one could be jealousy over my relationship with Jessica." Matt looked in her direction.

"Could those two reasons somehow involve the same people? That would support the theory that the three men acted together. Otherwise, we may have two sets of suspects." Sheriff White looked around at all of them and paused for a few seconds. "In any case, the first thing we need to do is to identify those individuals. It looks like you recognized one. Could you confirm it?"

"I'll talk to him." Jessica's voice was firm.

"I'll go with you, " Matt added, and Josh also offered to join.

"I don't think that he will talk if we all gang up on him. If this was a reaction to the moment, I think I can get him to admit it if I'm alone with him." Jessica's tone didn't leave any room for discussion.

"Okay, I agree," the sheriff stared at Matt, "and I'll try to identify the other two individuals. Skiers usually rent their equipment, and we only have four shops in the village, so I'll go visit them and show the images to see if anybody recognizes them."

"It sounds like a plan, Sheriff. Let's keep in touch and share what we find," Matt stood up and shook hands with the sheriff.

"Glad you're doing well. Next time, we'll talk some more about DB Corp. It's something that has bothered me for years, and we may have a shared interest."

"We'll be glad to share our views on their operations." Josh's eyes beamed.

On the way back to town, they revisited what they had found and the sheriff's comments. All agreed that if Tyler had been involved, it was unlikely that he would have coordinated something with the other two skiers. The altercation between Matt and Tyler had happened a few hours before the accident, so it would have been difficult for Tyler to develop a plan and find two people willing to participate in such a short time.

Chapter 17

J ESSICA SHARED THE information they got at Crystal Mountain with her father.

"I can't believe Tyler could have done something like that," John's eyes were on fire, "putting the life of another person at risk can't be justified by jealousy or rage, especially by someone who has a high-level education. We need to talk to Frank. Remember he told us on Monday that Tyler was going out of town for some time? I bet he knows and told his son to hide." He stood up and began to pace the room. "But we'll force him to come back and give us an explanation."

Jessica's eyes went wide. "And how are we going to do that?"

"We'll tell him that there is a video that compromises Tyler's situation."

LATER IN THE morning, John and Jessica walked into Frank's office, who received them with a smile.

"Good morning. It looks like something is bothering you. I hope Matt is doing okay."

"Yes, he's fine, Frank," Jessica answered dryly.

"Frank, we've something serious to discuss." John looked at him and pointed at the table in the office. "May we?"

"Of course," Frank got up with a smirk, "let's see what's so important you want to talk about." He leaned back in the chair with his arms crossed.

John put his hands on the table. "You mentioned that Tyler is going to be out of town for a while."

"Yes, he decided to visit some friends in New York."

"It's rather unusual for him to leave so suddenly when we have so much work to do at the firm. Is he hiding from something?"

"What do you mean?" Frank's face flushed.

Jessica decided to intervene. "We went with Matt to the mountain to help him try to remember something about the incident and also saw some videos from the cameras at the top of the mountain."

Frank opened his hands. "And?"

"We saw three individuals going down the slope after Matt. One of them on a snowboard looks like Tyler. He had on a blue parka, but the goggles prevented us from having a clear shot at his face; however, we all agree that it had to be Tyler."

"You know he was at the mountain that same day, don't you?"

Jessica's eyes narrowed. "Yes, but Matt remembers two guys led him to a black slope. When they left after making a threat, another person on a snowboard almost ran into him, making Matt lose control and run into the tree."

"So, you think that my son had something to do with Matt's accident? That's *absurd*. Why would he do that?" Frank got up and walked toward the window with his hands in his pockets.

John also got up and stood next to him. "Because earlier that afternoon Tyler and Matt had a disagreement when your son tried to accuse Matt of cheating on Jessica with another woman who turned to be a long-time friend."

Frank thought for a moment and then met John's eyes. "Look, those are discussions between young people trying to solve their problems, especially when two men are interested in the same girl. Now, creating a soap-opera story about Tyler trying to hurt Matt while skiing is a long stretch."

"Maybe he'll answer in court." John pointed at Frank.

"You know you don't have anything against him. A video of a skier with some resemblance to Tyler and Matt's story about someone on a snowboard getting too close on the slope—the most you could hope for is an accusation of reckless behavior against

Tyler, and that's assuming you can prove he was the individual who got too close to Matt."

"And that's why I want to talk to Tyler to see what he has to say." Jessica moved closer with her palms up, trying to calm down the two partners. "We've known each other for a long time, and I want to understand what happened. Maybe he saw the other two men who threatened Matt. I called Tyler, but he's not answering, and you mentioned he might not come back for some time. Do you have any way to contact him?"

"He's staying with some friends but sometimes calls. I'll explain to him why you're trying to reach him."

"I'd appreciate it, Frank. I hope he calls me."

Jessica and her father left the office.

"He knows what Tyler did." John shook his fist.

FRANK PICKED UP the phone. "Hi, Don, I want to alert you that the police are investigating Matt's incident, and there is a video with two suspects who they will try to identify."

Don Brackman lowered his head and closed his eyes for a few seconds. "That's what concerns me. I told those guys just to scare him a little. Do you know if they have any clues on who they may be?"

"Don't think so. Just be careful that nothing

points in your direction. If the police locate them, just instruct those guys to deny the whole thing. There is no evidence of the incident, and it would be Matt's words against theirs."

"Okay, thanks, Frank. Let me know if you find anything else."

THE NEXT PHONE call was to his son. "Tyler, everything okay down there?"

"Yes, Dad, spending time with friends. How about the situation on your side?"

"Just had a discussion with John and Jessica. She, Matt, and their friends went to the mountain to help him try to remember what happened the day of the accident and met with the police to analyze some videos."

Tyler's voice quivered. "And did he remember anything?"

"They think they saw you going down the mountain after Matt. They also saw two skiers beginning their run after Matt and in front of you. Do you remember them?"

"Yes, I saw three skiers going down together. I thought they were friends."

"It looks like Matt was one of them. Did you see whether the other two skiers threatened Matt before you got closer to him?"

"Was it Matt? I didn't notice anything. As I said, it looked to me that the two skiers caught up with who we assume was Matt, joined him for a while, and then skied off."

"And that's when you slid by him?"

"Yes. I wanted to speed past Matt but took a turn too fast and got too close to him."

"Why did you do that? Anything to do with the altercation you had earlier on with Matt?"

"Dad, I admit that I was mad but wouldn't try to make him crash into a tree."

Frank noticed his son's heavy breathing. "And you didn't see the crash?"

"No. I just regained control after getting too close to the skier and sped down because it was getting late."

"Okay. Jessica is trying to contact you to ask about the incident. John was threatening to present civil charges, but I think I defused that idea. My opinion is that you should talk to Jessica and describe what you just told me. I suggest not saying that you recognized Matt but describing the three skiers running the slopes together. There is no evidence or video of the incident, so they can't prove anything, and the most someone could accuse you is of going down too fast and being a little reckless."

"Should I come back to town?"

"I don't see why not. Your story is that you took a couple of days off to see some friends in New York.

You were not aware that Matt had suffered any injury until I told you and didn't answer Jessica's calls because you were having fun with your friends out of town."

"Okay, Dad. I'll head home and call Jessica to tell her that we can meet when I'm back in town."

TYLER WAS WAITING at the Newark airport to return home when his phone rang.

"Hello, Tyler? This is Rachel Avila, one of Matt's friends. We didn't have the opportunity to talk, but you took some pictures of Matt and me at a café."

"Oh, yes. Sorry, it was a big misunderstanding. I thought…"

"Stop. You don't need to apologize."

"But," Tyler looked at his phone's screen, searching for an answer, "I thought Jessica, Matt, and all of you were mad at me for that."

She giggled. "Oh, yes, they are not happy with you for sending those photos and video. But for me, it's different."

He pinched the bridge of his nose while closing his eyes. "I don't understand. Could you clarify why you're calling me?"

"Because we have a common interest, and I think we can help each other."

"Excuse me, but I don't see what we may have in common. What am I missing here?"

"You like Jessica, right? And wouldn't you like to try to get Matt out of her mind?"

Tyler saw a possible catch here trying to make him admit that he tried to hurt Matt. "I wish that she would forget Matt, but I wouldn't do anything to hurt him if that's what you're suggesting." He raised the tone of his voice.

"No. I'm not trying to suggest that. I would also like to see their relationship end."

Tyler's eyes went wide and, after a few seconds, he reacted to what he'd heard. "Are you saying that you're interested in Matt, and that's why you would help me to gain Jessica's heart?"

"*Bingo.* Do you see now that we have something in common?"

"Yes, I do." He couldn't contain his excitement. "Do you have a plan?"

"That's what I would like to discuss with you. I believe it should begin by you apologizing to Jessica and Matt for what happened. You could say that you went too fast down the slope, still upset after the discussion you'd had earlier in the day, and at one point remember getting too close to a skier but didn't realize that it caused an accident. Later, when you learned about Matt's accident through your father, you realized the skier could have been Matt."

"That story is like what my dad told me to say. Look, I'm in Newark, waiting for my flight back.

They're boarding now, and I need to go, but I'll call you when I arrive. Perhaps we can meet tomorrow?"

"Perfect. I'll be waiting to hear from you."

Chapter 18

JESSICA, MATT, RACHEL, and Josh got together for breakfast at the Border Café. Rachel and Matt missed the taste of Southern cuisine they enjoyed while growing up and suggested the place that had a simple atmosphere but outstanding food. They wanted to share the latest information regarding the incident at Crystal Mountain.

Jessica held a cup of coffee in her hand. "I talked to Tyler over the phone, and he was very apologetic. He admitted being at the mountain late that afternoon and having a close call when temporarily losing his control and almost running into a skier. He claims to have had no idea that it was Matt. He was upset after the argument earlier that afternoon and wasn't as careful as he usually is but swore he wouldn't try to hurt anybody. He got back from New York last night, where he spent time with friends, trying to forget the argument. Tyler wants to apologize in person to Matt and suggested joining him tonight for dinner."

"I don't believe a word," Josh mumbled while busy working on his huevos rancheros.

"Why not?" Rachel was holding her fork as a pointer. "After all, he and Jessica have been friends for a long time, and maybe his trip to New York helped him to reflect and accept that Jessica loves Matt."

"I don't know." Matt shook his head. "It seems very convenient. Maybe he thinks he has a shot at being with Jessica again and is just trying to play nice."

"I don't think so." Jessica gave Matt a sweet look. "He doesn't have a chance, and besides that, it sounded sincere. I think we should accept his invitation and see him in person before passing any judgment."

"Okay." Matt cleaned his mouth with a napkin and smiled at her. "Let's meet him and see what he has to say. I can always use a free dinner."

"I've also some news." Rachel grinned.

Josh leaned forward. "It must be something exciting."

"It is. I talked to Sheriff White, and he had some information about the identity of the two guys who threatened Matt."

"Now I'm all ears." Matt stared at her.

"As the sheriff said, they went to the local ski

shops and showed the employees pictures of the two guys in the videos. And it worked!"

Matt slammed the table with his hand. "We finally get a break. Have they identified those men?"

"The ski shop manager remembered them because they rented the skis that afternoon and used them for just a couple of hours which is pretty unusual. They returned the skis late afternoon right after the slopes closed."

"Does the sheriff have names?" Josh fidgeted.

"Yes. When renting skis, you provide personal information and leave an ID. The renter receives the ID back, but the shop keeps the personal information in their records. The police are verifying the names now and will try to locate them. It shouldn't take too long to be able to talk to them."

"That's *fantastic*." Matt raised his orange juice glass. "Cheers."

"We'll get them, Matt," Rachel clinked glasses, "but now I need to go. Someone is waiting for me."

"I'm jealous." Josh rubbed his eyes.

Rachel stood up and winked at him. "You're a clown."

When Rachel left, Josh stared at Matt.

"We need to decide what to do next. What the sheriff is doing sounds great, but what are we going to do with DB Corp.? Now that they have announced the investment in wastewater control, the PNA will lose interest in investigating them and especially with

Peterson on their side. The question is whether they could have been after you, and I believe we need to keep looking into their motivation and what's going on behind the scenes—something's not right."

"And don't forget about Brian—he found something that maybe was related to the fire in their facilities." Matt stretched on his chair.

A puzzled look came across Jessica's face. "Do you think they might have set fire to their facilities to collect insurance money?"

"It's a possibility, but that happened more than fifteen years ago, so why would they worry about us getting close to the brewery operation now?"

"Don't know, but if there was a premeditated fire, I'm sure the statute of limitations has long expired." Josh shook his head. "It has to be something else."

"Okay. We need to focus on the next steps." Matt leaned forward and made eye contact with both. "Let's talk with Brian's sister, Beth, again and try to find out more about his whereabouts before his accident. Josh, would you join me? Also, we may want to pay a second visit to Mario Ramirez. Maybe he knows someone else who worked at the plant at that time. Hopefully, we can gather some additional information while we wait for Sheriff White to complete his investigation."

"I can talk to my father, too. I believe he's becoming more and more suspicious about his partner's relationship with DB Corp. and may be able to help." Jessica tilted her head.

"Just make sure he's comfortable helping us. He has a long-standing relationship with Frank and DB Corp. and may get defensive if we suggest that we'll keep investigating them beyond the wastewater issue."

"I'll make sure he understands what we're trying to do. Since your accident, he's been open to considering irregularities in the brewery operation and his partner's potential involvement. It's in his self-interest. If there *is* something wrong, he doesn't want to be involved in it."

"Remember that we also have the material Rachel found in Channel 5's archives."

"That's right" Matt's eyes sparkled. "It looks like we have plenty of work to do."

Jessica couldn't contain her anxiety while clenching Matt's arm. "But please be careful if you go back to Miscales. Remember, it could be dangerous, and I'm worried about you."

TYLER WAS PACING in the living room of his apartment when the bell rang. He almost ran over a coffee table when rushing to open the door.

"Rachel, nice to meet you. I appreciate you coming to my place." He had seen her at a distance talking to Matt the evening he had taken the pictures, but now he was impressed with her beauty.

"Nice to meet you, too, Tyler. You have a great place. It is very convenient to meet here so nobody will see us together." She walked into the living room, admiring the large window with a view of the bay and the stylish furniture. He invited her to sit on a white leather sofa.

"Can I offer you a drink?" He couldn't avoid noticing her stunning body highlighted by a tight button-front white top and brown leather pants. *Wow, she's beautiful. I can imagine Jessica's jealousy when she saw the pictures.*

"I just had breakfast with Jessica, Matt, and Josh, so the only thing I need is a glass of water. Thanks."

"Okay, but you need to give me a raincheck for real drinks." He waggled his brows.

Rachel giggled. "We'll see. We need to focus now on developing a plan."

Tyler walked into the spacious open-concept kitchen and returned with a glass of water and a beer before sitting next to her. "Tell me more about your relationship with Matt."

She gazed at him while playing with her hair. "It's a long story. We grew up as neighbors and spent a lot of time together. I had a crush on him, and we had a fling, but he's older than me and was into other things. Then my family moved to a different town and lost contact. About ten days ago, Josh invited me to meet with a friend working on something that could be of interest to my TV station. I didn't know the person was Matt, and we had a good time reminiscing. Seeing him in front of me caused my feelings as a teenager to come back. I had never forgotten him."

"And do you think he felt the same for you?"

"When I walked into the café where he was waiting, his gaze went all over me, and when he stood up, he almost spilled his coffee. Matt mentioned that he's been dating Jessica, but I noticed he was a little uncomfortable when talking about her."

"Do you think they don't have a strong relationship?"

"I think it's quite strong, especially after Matt's accident and her being around him all the time while he recovered."

Tyler opened his hand. "How are we going to break it off?"

She touched his arm. "We've to be patient. I think if we can create some disappointment for Matt's behavior, Jessica would be vulnerable, and that would be your time to step in to be there for her."

"I've lost some points with the accident." He looked down and tapped his fingers.

"That's okay. You have to pretend to be her best friend, supportive, and happy with her relationship with Matt. I've gained her confidence, and she looks at me as one of her best friends now."

Tyler shook his head. "You know that in addition to being beautiful, you have a mischievous mind?"

Rachel took a sip of water and wet her lips with her tongue. "I have many attributes and skills."

"Are you sure you have feelings for Matt, or is it a sort of revenge for not paying attention to you when you had a crush on him?"

She smiled. "Now that you mention it, I'm not sure, but that shouldn't bother you if you get Jessica, right?"

He looked at his beer for a moment, swirling the bottle around. "I guess not. Do you have any specific plan?"

"First, you're going to see Matt and Jessica at dinner this evening. She believed your story that it was an unfortunate incident when you were going down too fast and didn't know the person you almost crashed into was Matt. He is not convinced, and that's why you must make a believable argument today. Remember you're happy about their relationship and want to support them as a friend."

"And what do we do next?"

"I thought we could come up with ideas together. Do you know of any situation or other people who could help us?"

"Jessica's mom. She doesn't think Matt's good enough for her and let me know that I would be a good option for her daughter. I understand she tried to talk against a promotion for Matt at the school."

"*Excellent.* Do you think we can enlist her to be on our side?"

"I would need to check since I don't know whether the situation with the accident has changed her opinion."

"You could probably talk with her parents and say that it was an unfortunate coincidence, and you didn't have any intention to hurt Matt. You have to convince them that you're sorry about the whole incident. And hopefully, you can find out whether Mrs. Dalton still sees you in a good light."

"I can do that."

"Is there anything that you know that Jessica doesn't like about Matt's activities or personality?"

"I think she supports him but is not totally on board with his activities with the PNA. She thinks he spends too much time on environmentalist stuff and he may get into trouble by trying to help others or going after lost causes."

"Good to know. I'll try to get Jessica to talk about it."

"Wow. I'm exhausted with all this brainstorming." Tyler rolled his head from side to side.

She got closer to him and looked into his eyes. "Maybe we should release the tension now. Do you have some music? I could use that drink you offered."

Tyler grinned. "You're full of surprises. Of course, I can offer drinks and music." He took the remote control, and "Perfect" began playing.

"Ed Sheridan, one of my favorites." She got up and began to dance slowly.

He got up, put his arm around her waist, and pressed her against his body while catching up with the dance. They continued dancing without saying a word.

Tyler looked at her beautiful eyes. "Are you sure you're interested in Matt?"

"As much as you're interested in Jessica," she smiled, "but it doesn't prevent us from having a good time, does it?"

He stopped moving. "Certainly not," and softly kissed her lips which she returned with passion. He tried to push her back to the sofa, but she pushed him away, giggling. "Not so fast. It's nice to have a drink and chat a little first."

Tyler was confused by her behavior. *Why flirt with me in my apartment while trying to break apart her friend's relationship?* "How about some champagne?"

"It's sort of early for that, but why not?" Rachel played with the buttons of her V-neck top and took the glass offered to her. "Cheers. To the success of our plan."

He winked at her. "Looking forward to more meetings like this."

"This meeting's not over yet." She touched the champagne with her finger and put it on his lips.

Tyler felt aroused and sucked her finger while bringing her body closer. He was burning with desire, and so was she. They kissed again, and when he lifted her, Rachel felt like she was swirling into the stars, and her body trembled in anticipation of what was coming. She hadn't planned this, but she had learned to follow her impulses and enjoy the moment.

A few hours later, she came out of the bedroom and picked up her clothes scattered around the living room like the remnants of a battle. And what a battle it had been. Two bodies intertwined in a continuous and frenetic quest to provide and feel the pleasure that began their love wrestling on the sofa and had moved through the room while shedding their clothes and ended in the bedroom.

Tyler came after her, pouting. "Are we done already?"

"It was wonderful, but I've got things to do at the station, and remember you have to attend dinner with Jessica and Matt."

"Okay, okay, but promise that we'll do it again."

Rachel turned and made eye contact without blinking. "Remember, we agreed to enjoy the moment but shouldn't lose focus on our goal. You're after Matt to get Jessica back. We may or may not repeat that, depending on whether you take it as it is—no commitments." She finished dressing and went for the door.

Chapter 19

MATT AND JOSH went to Beth Oliver's townhouse in First Hill, a popular neighborhood for young professionals. She was expecting them after receiving Matt's call that morning and agreed to meet the same day since she worked from home. Beth hugged them with affection, and the trio moved to the living area and sat on a loveseat and two dark-teal fabric armchairs. She had prepared some cookies and placed them on a tray on a white metal coffee table.

"Those look delicious." Josh bent over the coffee table, pretending to smell the cookies before sitting in one of the armchairs.

"I remember you and Brian were always fighting over who would take the last one." Her eyes clouded for an instant.

Matt leaned forward. "How have you managed since the accident? Are you doing okay?"

"It was hard at the beginning," she looked down

with a sad smile, "but I'm getting better. Focusing on my job helps a lot."

"Good. You need to keep your mind busy. May I?" Josh was already attacking the plate of cookies.

Matt kept eye contact with her. "We've been waiting to talk but tried to give you some time to soften the grief. I hate to sound callous, but we'd like to know whether Brian shared anything about what he was investigating on DB Corp. We're trying to continue what he was doing and need any information you may have. His death looks suspicious to us."

Beth's eyes went wide open. "Do you think someone caused his accident? Sometimes I think it's bizarre that he was run over while jogging. Brian was careful and safety conscious."

Josh used a paper napkin to clean up some crumbs. "It looks like he found something and was trying to share it when he said, *Tell Matt the fire*. We think he was referring to a fire that caused a lot of damage at the brewery about fifteen years ago. Did he mention anything to you before his accident?"

"He was upset with the way DB Corp. ran their operations and had a feeling that the brewery business hid something. The day before the accident, he was thrilled about something he had found."

"Do you know whether he talked to anyone that could have shared information?"

She bit her lip and scratched her temple for a few seconds. "Brian mentioned something about a fireman who was willing to share a story, but he didn't give me any details."

Matt looked at Josh. "*The fire!*" and turning back to Beth. "Did he mention the name of that person?"

She shook her head. "Sorry, I don't remember the guy's name."

"Did he say where he met him?"

"No, but I know the day before the accident, he went to Miscales."

Josh shrugged. "It looks like we need to talk to Mr. Ramirez again."

"You're right. It looks like we'll get some answers in that town."

"Do you think Brian's finding triggered something against him?" Beth's breathing quickened.

"It's too soon to say that, but we'll look into it and let you know. We better go now. Sorry to bring up sad memories, Beth. If there is anything else you remember, please let us know even if it seems insignificant."

She got up and led them to the door. "I will. And you keep me posted."

TYLER ARRIVED AT Spinasse—a well-known Italian restaurant—a little early to make sure they would get a table in a corner to have some privacy. Around fifteen minutes later, Jessica and Matt came in the front door and waved.

They are smiling. Maybe it's not going to be too bad. Tyler stood up to greet them as they moved closer to the table. The light snow covering the street and blanketing the trees gave them a topic for some casual conversation until Tyler looked at Matt.

"I know we have not had a friendly relationship, especially the last time we saw each other at the mountain.

Matt shrugged. "No need to go back through that now."

"I want to because I owe you an apology. That day I was angry because I thought you were cheating on Jessica."

She gave Matt a sweet look and caught his hand.

"But I know better now. The time I took with my friends in New York made me see the truth and believe me when I say I'm happy for both of you."

"It's sweet of you to say that." Jessica put her head on Matt's shoulder.

"It's the way I feel, and Matt, I want to apologize. My anger made me race down the hill recklessly, and I almost lost control when going by a skier that I know now was you. I didn't realize that I caused an accident. I was too focused on myself, and I'm sorry for what happened."

Matt waved his hand. "Tyler, I appreciate your invitation today and your apology. It's not the first time rage has caused an accident. What's important is that we're all here. Let's enjoy the meal. How was your visit to New York?"

"Thank you, Matt. Seeing my friends was good and helped a lot."

"Are you considering going back there to work?"

"Not really. That crossed my mind, but then I decided that my place is to stay here with my father's firm."

The waiter interrupted to take their order.

"The risotto al fungi and the seared salmon with toasted pumpkin seeds are great here," Tyler suggested with a smile.

Jessica looked at Matt. "Do you want to order one each and share?"

"How can I say no to a beautiful lady?"

"Done deal," Tyler closed the menu and looked at the waiter, "and for me, the roasted rabbit meatballs with caramelized onions."

"Oh," Jessica pouted, "how dare you eat bunnies?"

"I'll let you try some," grinned Tyler, "and maybe you'll decide to switch plates."

"Never," she said, and as Matt smiled, she turned to him with a pointed finger, "and don't you think about eating rabbits."

"Okay, darling, I promise."

The conversation continued over dinner in a very relaxed atmosphere, sharing their latest activities.

"So, Matt, is the PNA satisfied with DB Corp. investing in water treatment facilities?" Tyler asked casually while finishing his plate.

"The PNA president certainly is, but some of us still think there's something fishy behind DB Corp. operations."

"How so?" Tyler's furrowed brow gave up his surprise at the comment.

"There was a fire at the brewery many years ago that was not investigated as it should have, then a friend of mine who found some important information died in a hit-and-run, and two guys tried to scare me just before my accident. Too many coincidences if you ask me."

"Are you saying that those two guys skiing with you on the day of the accidents were threatening you?"

"Yes. Did you see them?"

"I saw a skier that I now realize was you, joined by two guys skiing together for a while until those two moved ahead."

Jessica's eyes went wide open. "Could you recognize those guys?"

"I'm afraid not. Everything happened too fast. Sorry."

Matt leaned back on his chair. "Don't worry. Sheriff White from Crystal County has done a good job in identifying those two."

"That's good. Have they been questioned?"

"Not yet, but the police are trying to locate them. The sheriff is interested in a possible connection with DB Corp. He's still suspicious about the company's ethics based on his personal experience at the time of the brewery fire."

"Wow, and all this started with your work with the PNA?"

Jessica looked down while twisting her ring. "We think so."

"When things begin escalating between business and those environmental groups, some violence usually happens." Tyler frowned.

"That's what I told Matt, but he's so committed to the PNA." She grabbed Matt's arm.

"Because I believe there's something wrong with the operation of that brewery. Once we get to the bottom of it, I promise I will focus one hundred percent on my teaching career."

"It sounds like it'll make you both happy. A toast to that." Tyler raised his glass and then kept talking about his intention to strengthen his father's law firm.

After sharing a delicious tiramisu with Spinasse's famous Italian coffee, they left the restaurant.

"It's been a nice evening, Tyler. Thanks for the invitation." Jessica hugged him.

"My pleasure and I'm glad that we got to know each other better, Matt. Sorry again about the misunderstanding and the whole accident."

Matt extended his hand. "It's all in the past. This place was a great choice, and the food was delicious."

Matt and Jessica were driving back home, and she turned to him. "Do you think he was sincere?"

He tilted his head and raised his eyebrows. "Tyler was certainly relaxed and seemed to be interested in how we're doing. I didn't see the jealousy over our relationship that he showed a few weeks ago."

"As he said, maybe the break to visit his friends helped him to face reality and understand that he could be my friend but nothing else."

Matt took her hand. "I hope so."

Tyler called Rachel to share that dinner had gone according to plan and then phoned his father.

"Hi, Dad. I just finished having dinner with Jessica and Matt, and I think you might want to know a few things I found out."

"Okay. Why don't you come to the office early in the morning and we can talk?"

"I'll do but make sure it's just the two of us and John isn't around."

Chapter 20

TYLER KNOCKED AT the door of his father's office. "Hi, Dad. It looks like you're interested in the news."

Frank left the paper on his desk and waved him in. "Tell me more about your dinner last night. Did you enjoy it?"

"Yes. I'm trying to get on Jessica and Matt's good side. But I heard something that I'm sure will interest you."

His father tilted his head. "What is it?"

"We were talking about Matt's accident, and they mentioned that the Crystal County Sheriff was able to identify the two skiers who threatened Matt just before the accident."

"How so? Who are they?"

"Don't know yet, but the sheriff is looking for them. Furthermore, Matt and his friend will continue to search for evidence against DB Corp."

Frank's creased brows showed his dislike. "I thought they were interested in the wastewater issue. What are they looking for now?"

"Matt believes there's a connection between the fire at the brewery and the death of his friend, Brian Oliver, a couple of months ago. It looks like Brian wanted to share something he discovered related to the brewery fire when he was run over by a car."

"But that was an accident."

"Matt doesn't think it was an accident and also believes that the threats from those two guys were related to his brewery investigations."

Frank got up from his chair and raised a fist. "That idiot wants to play detective and doesn't know what he's getting into."

Tyler shrugged. "Why do we care?"

Frank's thoughts went back to his beginnings in San Diego when he dealt with border issues and met some dark characters. That was also when he got to know Don Brackman and became the lawyer for his corporation. He looked at his son and wiggled a pointing finger. "You don't need to know."

Tyler froze and stared at his father with wide eyes. "What? I thought you would share everything about our firm and especially about our largest client."

"Believe me; you don't need to know." Putting his hand over his son's shoulder and making unblinking eye contact, he added. "I'm protecting you."

"*Protecting me*?" Tyler raised his eyebrows and

pointed at his chest but looking at his dad's firm gaze, he stood up and left the office, looking down and shaking his head.

Frank stood with both fists on his desk and breathing heavily. *That idiot, Don Brackman, tried to save a few bucks by not investing in water treatment, and now we have everybody wanting to investigate the brewery operation.* He paced around the room while rubbing the nape of his neck. *We need to stop this.* He picked up the phone.

"Don, we need to talk."

Don Brackman noticed the distress in his lawyer's voice. "Is there a problem?"

"Yes, and you better do something to fix it. The police identified those two guys you sent to threaten Matt Hernandez and are looking for them."

"They're hiding…"

"*Bullshit*," Frank barked. "Unless they're at the other end of the world, it's a question of time before they're caught and made to talk."

"Listen, these guys know how to hide."

"And that's not all," Frank interrupted again. "Matt and his friend will continue to look into the brewery fire because they assume there is a connection between that and the accidents that took the life of Brian Oliver and injured Matt. By the way, the sheriff of Crystal County was one of the police involved at the time of the fire and is not convinced that there was a proper investigation."

There was silence on the other side of the line until Don said in a gravelly voice, "It looks like the threats didn't work, and we'll need to take more drastic measures."

"You do whatever you have to, but we can't allow new investigations into it. Our partners will be upset." Frank's tone sounded like a warning.

"I know. Let me plan something."

"Better than planning, take some action and *quickly*." Frank hung up and returned to his desk. *How am I going to tell our partners that the operation is in danger of being discovered?* He ran his hands through his hair.

Josh and Matt were driving under a steady drizzle to see Mario Ramirez in Miscales. They saw the sign for the secondary road going to the small town but continued on the main road.

"Where is the place Mario mentioned?" Matt was getting impatient to meet with their contact.

"He said to take the next exit and stop at the fast-food restaurant on the right. It has a back door. We should go through it and get into a blue VW that will be parked there. Then we'll need to drive eight miles to the town of Blue River where he'll be waiting for us."

"Is he scared?"

"A couple of guys went to his house after the last time we were with him and reminded Mario of his promise not to talk about the brewery fire. So, this time he wants to make sure nobody will follow us."

Matt rubbed his hand. "This is another sign that we're getting closer to finding something big."

"But it also means we have to be careful. We're playing with some rough people." Josh looked at his friend with worried eyes.

They parked at the restaurant, and Matt elbowed Josh while his eyes looked at a truck approaching the parking lot. "We better hurry to get into the blue car."

They moved quickly and were driving out when they saw two men casually getting out of the truck and walking into the restaurant while one of them was talking on the phone.

Matt drove fast, checking that nobody was following them, and got to the Blue River exit in a little more than five minutes. Josh did the navigation, following Mario's instructions. Soon they arrived at a small white house with a porch where a bike and some toy trucks and frisbees scattered around the front yard indicated the presence of children. The doorbell ringing brought to the door a smiling face with beautiful green eyes and chubby cheeks chewing on a candy bar.

"Hi, we're looking for Mario Ramirez." Matt bent down to meet the eyes of the little boy.

"*Grandpa!* Two guys are here for you." And he ran inside.

"Always tell them not to open to strangers, but who can control kids?" Mario said while looking to both sides of the street. "Are you sure nobody followed you? Please come in."

"We followed your instructions. It was a good idea to switch vehicles. We lost the guys who followed us from town," Josh reassured their host.

"I know. You may not have noticed, but a green truck was parked next to the VW at the restaurant. The VW is my daughter's car, and my son-in-law was in the truck to make sure you got it and delay those guys if they realized that you went through the back door. This is their house, and I thought it would be safer to see you here."

"Good planning, Mario. We appreciate you agreeing to meet with us again."

"Those thugs scared me last time, but I want to help you."

"Mario, did you have time to possibly identify the fireman who was involved in the brewery fire and shared anything about it with our friend, Brian Oliver?"

"These are small towns, and everybody knows everybody around here, so I asked some questions and believe I know who that person may have been."

"Do you have his address? Could we talk to him?" Matt interrupted while pumping a fist in the air.

"Better than that." Mario smiled. "He'll be here in a few minutes. I called him when I saw you pull up at the house."

"You're great, Mario!"

Josh clapped Mario's shoulder. "We appreciate this."

"Not sure if he's the same guy who talked to your friend, but he was at the fire and shared the same views I have in terms of it being a suspicious incident."

At that point, someone knocked on the door, and Mario's daughter let him in. A fifty-something-year-old, tall man with peppered hair and broad shoulders came into the room and shook hands with Mario.

"Gentlemen, this is Paul Benitez, the person I think you want to talk to."

Matt extended his hand. "Hello, Mr. Benitez. Thanks for coming."

"Please, call me Paul. Mario told me you're interested to know more about the refinery fire."

"Yes, and we would like to know whether you met Brian Oliver, a friend of ours, a few weeks ago about this same topic."

"I did."

Matt and Josh shared a smile.

"He came asking questions about the fire, and I shared my concerns that the official report of the investigation was not fully accurate."

Matt's eyes narrowed. "Are you aware that Brian died in a suspicious accident the next day?"

Paul stared with wide eyes while Mario blew out

his cheeks, and his daughter, who was still around, held her hands over her mouth.

"I told you, Dad, that you should forget all about it." She hugged her dad while sending an icy look to Matt and Josh.

"Okay, baby. Nothing is going to happen. Let's go to the other room and let these gentlemen talk." Mario put his hand behind his daughter's back, and they walked out.

"Sorry. Didn't want to scare anybody," Matt apologized.

"There must be something big hidden behind that fire. Some of us never understood why the police ignored so much evidence," Paul said with a flinch.

Josh leaned forward. "Evidence? What sort of evidence?"

"When we arrived at the brewery, the fire had expanded quickly from the lab to the warehouse. There were also some explosions at the lab. We didn't expect that from a brewery lab since they usually don't handle volatile material in large volumes."

"Did you figure out the cause of the explosions?" Matt interrupted.

"Drums of flammable material. And there was an acid smell also. We reported it, but the police report ignored it."

"Wasn't the cause of the fire identified as an electrical short?"

"That was the official word but not what our investigators said."

Josh's crinkled nose encouraged Paul to continue.

"The thought was that an explosion happened while handling flammable material. The embers from drum explosions caused the rapid expansion of the fire that engulfed the lab and reached the warehouse."

"You mentioned that the investigators ignored some evidence. What was it?" Matt gazed at him in astonishment.

"First, the explosions that ignited several drums were at the lab. Why would a quality control lab store flammable materials instead of keeping them at the warehouse? Second, there was a strong smell like rotten eggs that may have been associated with the presence of ammonia. Sometimes ammonia is used in the refrigeration processes, but the lab didn't have refrigeration where the fire started. The lab had two sections. The first one for quality control and the second one for research and development. The fire started in the second section."

"How could those leads be ignored?"

"As I mentioned, management provided answers, but nothing was subject to an in-depth analysis. The explanations, in my view, were weak. And there's more…."

"*More?*" Josh raised his eyebrows.

"I found a few drum lids with product identi-fication. MEK, hydrochloric acid, and acetic anhydride. Not sure why the brewery used those materials, but nobody wanted to investigate at that time. I mentioned this to Brian, and he was going to follow up. After his visit, I went to my attic and found the lids from the fire."

"I can see why Brian was so excited about what he'd learned." Matt's mind went back to the last conversation with his friend, and he felt sad. "Paul, this has been useful, and we'll share it with a friend of ours who runs a lab. He may be able to help us get some answers."

They kept talking until Mario came back with his daughter. "It looks like you found some interesting things to chat about." He smiled.

"Yes, thanks for your help. We would like to ask you one more thing."

"What is it?"

"You know a lot of people around here, and I assume some would still be working at the brewery?"

"That's right. Some operators began their careers before I retired, and I used to mentor a few of them. Great guys. Some of them made it to supervisors."

"Do you think they might consider helping us in our investigations?"

"I'm pretty sure they will because nobody is happy with how things are managed there."

"Great. We would need your friends inside the brewery to keep a close eye on the operations. As this investigation keeps making progress, we're not sure how they will react, especially if there's something to hide."

"I see your point. We'd all like to have some answers, so we'll be your eyes and let you know if anything out of the ordinary happens."

"Thanks. We better keep moving now and figure out how to lose those guys who followed us." Matt stood up.

"Don't worry. Those crooks aren't at the restaurant any longer." Mario laughed while he winked at Paul and noticed Josh and Matt exchanging glances. "My cousin owns the restaurant. Let's say he prepared some extra spicy tacos for those guys. After a few runs to the bathroom, they didn't have a choice but to leave." Now everybody was shaking with laughter. "My son-in-law will drive you back to get your truck."

"It's better to have you as a friend, Mario." Matt tilted his head while shaking hands.

They went through the employees' door in the back of the restaurant and confirmed what Mario had said. Josh jumped into the driver's seat. "Should we stop by to see Oscar on the way back home?"

"Definitely, my friend. I'm sure he can tell us more about those chemicals found in the fire."

During the trip, they revisited all the information provided by Paul and grew excited about the findings.

Matt tapped the dashboard enthusiastically. "This has been a fruitful visit."

"It certainly was." Josh smiled and, pointing to a small white building, added, "Here is the lab. Let see what Oscar tells us."

The lab technician was working with some test tubes and recording his observations when he saw them coming into the facility.

"You two must have something interesting. I can see the eagerness in your faces."

"Good observation, Oscar," Matt went for a high-five, "and we hope you'll help to make it even better."

"What's up, guys?"

"As you know, we're investigating the brewery operations."

"Are you bringing in some new water samples?" Oscar interrupted.

Josh's eyes brightened. "No, something different." The technician shrugged, and Josh continued, "There are indications that the investigation on the causes of brewery fire was very superficial, and a witness found damaged MEK, hydrochloric acid, and acetic anhydride's drum lids at the site. Does that tell you anything?"

Oscar frowned. "Those chemicals don't seem typical of a brewery operation."

"That's what we suspected." Matt clenched his hand above his head. "Why would they have them?"

Josh intervened, keeping eye contact with Oscar. "Do you know the main uses of these products?"

Seeing some doubts in the technician's eyes, he insisted, "Give us something to work on, even if it's just a hint."

The technician struck his chin and looked distantly for a few seconds. "MEK is a solvent used in coatings and other applications, but it's also an extraction medium."

"They justified the presence of MEK as a solvent for equipment cleaning."

"That's possible, but there are cheaper solvents for cleaning equipment. Why pay more?" Oscar was pacing the room now. "Hydrochloric acid is used in steel processing and the production of batteries. It's also used to process sugar and make gelatin."

Josh shook his head and offered a tight-lip smile, and Matt scratched his head while Oscar continued.

"Acetic anhydride is mostly used as a raw material for cellulose acetate fibers and in the manufacture of plastic, but it's also a key raw material for pharmaceuticals production like aspirin."

Matt shrugged. "This looks like a puzzle."

"But there is something they all have in common." Oscar looked at them. "Drug manufacturing." That got their attention, and he continued, "MEK can be used to produce cocaine and heroin, acetic anhydride is used to produce heroin from morphine, and hydrochloric acid is part of the process to make methamphetamines."

"Are you suggesting that somehow the labs were

used for the production of illegal substances?" Matt's eyes were wide open.

"I'm just saying that there is a common denominator that could justify the presence of those materials, and it's not exactly beer production."

"*Wow*." Josh smacked the palm of his hand against his forehead. "This is *big*. What are we going to do now*?*"

Matt stared at his friend. "First, we're going to calm down and try to validate it. Paul mentioned an unpleasant smell at the fire."

"That could be sulfuric acid, which is also used in the production of drugs," Oscar interrupted.

Matt raised his index finger. "Good. Now, why would someone try to hide an illegal drug operation inside a brewery?"

"Maybe Rachel or Sheriff White has contacts that can educate us?"

"Great idea, Josh. Let's share this information with them and see whether they think of something or know someone who can help us." Matt got up and motioned Josh to follow. "You're a genius, Oscar." And then they left the lab.

They were driving back to town and chatting excitedly about their findings when Matt's phone rang.

"Where have you been? Are you okay? I called all day and you never answered. I've been so worried about you." Jessica's quivering voice quenched his excitement.

"Sorry, Jess. It's been a hectic day, and I'm coming back to town with Josh now."

"And you couldn't call to let me know you were okay?" she snapped.

"I should have called, but we found a lot of new information…"

"I see where your priorities are. Your investigations first and I'm last," Jessica interrupted.

"Let me explain. I can stop by now. We're not far away."

"It's late, and I'm not in the mood." Jessica's dry answer didn't offer many options.

"Let's do something. We can get together tomorrow for lunch, and I'll explain."

"Not sure if I want to hear your explanation, Matt. Call me in the morning." And she hung up.

Matt's eyes were wide and staring into the road.

"What happened?" Josh looked at him.

"I just screwed up. Jessica's mad because I didn't respond to her calls all day."

"Maybe it's just a reaction. You'll see when you talk to her, everything is going to be fine."

"Not sure. Since my accident, she's been afraid and sensitive about our investigations on DB Corp."

Chapter 21

"WHAT DO YOU mean they've lost them?" Don Brackman barked over the phone. "Sir, we followed them as you requested. They drove in the direction of the brewery and turned at the first exit after Miscales."

"Isn't that the town they went to last time to talk to that Ramirez traitor?"

"Yes, but they didn't go into town. They stopped at a restaurant, and that's where our men lost them." Joe Brown's quavering voice gave away his embarrassment.

"*How?*"

"Our guys went into the restaurant, but they weren't there. Their truck was still parked outside, though."

"And what did they do?" Don Brackman's voice raised.

"They decided to wait and ordered some food to

avoid being noticed, but then got food poisoning and had to leave."

"*What*?" his frustration exploded like bubbles of champagne when uncorking a bottle.

"On the way back, they checked Ramirez's house, but they weren't there. My guys saw Hernandez and his friend returning to his apartment last night."

"That means those sissies you sent didn't do the job, and we don't know what they were doing around Miscales," Brackman shouted while holding the phone in front of him as if looking at Brown. "I don't want to see this type of failure repeated." And he hung up, throwing the phone onto the floor.

The noise of the phone crashing brought his assistant to the door. "Is everything okay, Mr. Brackman?"

"Yeah, the phone just slipped. Get me a new one and call Mr. Morris."

She knew to move quickly when her boss was in that kind of mood and had learned to keep a spare phone ready. Brackman's outbursts were becoming more frequent.

"Frank, we know Hernandez and his friend went to a small town not too far from the brewery yesterday. We think they're talking with people and looking for information related to the fire."

"I told you so. Have you decided what to do about it?" The lawyer's icy words pierced Brackman's rage.

"I think we need to update our partners on what's

going on and ask for their help to solve it. I can't allow any link between DB Corp. and what may happen to these guys who are putting their noses where they shouldn't."

Frank closed his eyes and pinched the bridge of his nose for an instant. "Maybe you're right. We can't continue hiding the situation from our partners. I don't know whether they would prefer to take action on those fake investigators or implement the emergency plan."

"The emergency plan implies some serious loss of income," Brackman tried to argue.

"Yes, but more *accidents* could bring additional investigations. You run the brewery, but it's their operation, so *they* will need to decide." Frank's tone conveyed a powerful message.

"Okay. Let me know the decision."

THE RESTAURANT HAD a nice view with sailboats dotting the bay like stars in a clear night. Jessica had finally agreed to get together for lunch, and Matt wanted to create the right environment. A beautiful bouquet with a dozen roses was in the chair next to him. She walked in, and her face changed to a tight-lipped smile when he offered her the flowers.

The roses were a good move. At least we made some progress. Matt kissed her on the cheek. "I wanted to apologize for my behavior yesterday. I should have called you," Matt began to say.

Jessica didn't say anything and just took the napkin and put it on her lap while looking through the window.

"I understand you're mad at me but let me tell you what happened. *Please*?"

She exhaled and looked at him with her chin resting on her fist. Matt described the meetings with the fireman and the retired brewery operator and the information gathered at the lab. His enthusiasm rose as the story progressed, and she just kept silent, looking at him until they were interrupted by the waiter offering drinks and appetizers. He ordered two shrimp cocktails—her favorite—and a bottle of rosé. Then kept his eyes on her.

"It seems to me that there's something more than a missed phone call. Is something else bothering you?"

Jessica's bewilderment at his question raised his concerns.

"Matt, you know I love you…."

He leaned forward. "I know, and I love you, too."

"I'm suffering a lot with your obsession with DB Corp. I understand that you were doing your job as a PNA member to pursue compliance with environmental regulations."

He tried to talk, but she raised her hand.

"But the company has agreed to make the

necessary investment and you keep investigating them."

He lowered his gaze and shook his head.

"And it's dangerous to do that. Remember your ski accident? And now you're telling me that it may also involve drug manufacturing?"

"That's precisely the point. This is bigger than environmental compliance. They should be held accountable for whatever they're doing and for Brian's death."

"We all have reasons to believe that they may have been involved in something criminal, but there's no proof. Why don't you let the police do their job?"

"Because the police didn't investigate the brewery fire and very quickly labeled Brian's death as an accident. DB Corp. is powerful and has connections everywhere. We'll find a way to prove it," he touted excitedly.

She put her elbows onto the table and squeezed her hands. "You see? All you care about is becoming a hero by proving some wrongdoing of a large corporation. What about us? Where am I in your priorities?" A tear rolled down her cheek. "I feel like I'm beating a dead horse here and I'm not going to take it any longer." Jessica put the flowers on the table and picked up her purse.

"Wait, Jessi. I told you that I love you."

"If that's so, you have to think how to behave accordingly, *Mr. Hernandez*." She turned around and left.

He sat perplexed, ignoring the looks of other guests who had noticed their argument. *What is this? I can't believe her reaction just for not calling yesterday. Is she trying to break up with me?* He asked for the check and slowly walked to the door while chewing on the words she had said.

While walking to his car, his phone rang. "Matt? This is Rachel. I found something that will interest you."

"Oh, hi, Rachel." His voice was quivering.

"What's wrong? Am I calling at a bad time?"

"No, no. Just a discussion over lunch."

"Do you want to tell me about it? You know you can count on me for whatever you need."

"Thanks, Rachel. What's up?"

"I did some research on the security cameras around the time of Brian's accident and found something I want you to see."

Matt's foggy thoughts cleared immediately. "What is it?"

"Better to watch it. I'm at home. If you want to stop by, we can analyze it together. Are you available? Maybe Josh, too."

"I can be there in about ten minutes, but Josh took advantage of the weekend to visit his parents."

She smiled; *I know. Josh told me, too.* "Great. See you then."

RACHEL LIVED IN a lovely fifth-floor apartment with a balcony that had a magnificent view of downtown and the mountains marking the horizon. At sunset, the sun's light turned the snowed peaks into a multi-color palette of red, orange, yellow, and white in contrast with the dark-green carpet of pine trees on the lower side of the mountains. This clear afternoon was going to be perfect, and she rubbed her hands in anticipation.

Matt couldn't avoid staring with wide eyes and raised eyebrows when she opened the door. Rachel was barefoot and wearing red shorts with a deep V-neck crop top that showed her flat tummy and highlighted her cleavage.

"Sorry, I'm pretty casual at home on weekends. Hope you don't mind." She smiled. Her beautiful blue eyes seemed brighter, accentuated by her olive skin and black hair tied back in a ponytail with a red band.

He froze for a few seconds and then grinned. "Don't mind at all. You look gorgeous anyway."

Rachel led him into the dining room that opened through a double-pane glass door onto the balcony.

"*Wow*. What a view." He put his hands over the rail, admiring the breathtaking panorama.

"And there is going to be a beautiful sunset in a couple of hours. Hope you can stay unless you have other plans."

Matt bowed his head, and his shoulders slumped

forward in disappointment. "I don't have any plans for this evening."

"You can't lie to me. We've known each other for a long time, and I can tell something's bothering you." She put her hand on his arm.

"Nothing. We better look at those videos now."

"As you wish. I'm sure it will cheer you up." Rachel took his hand and led him through the living room and into a small office.

A colonial-style desk with a mid-back mahogany chair were next to a window, and a laptop was open in the center of the desk. A pencil cup in the shape of an old-style typewriter, a blue mug with the words Write On in gold, and a smartphone video-rig kit with video light gave away that a journalist worked there. She invited him to sit in front of the laptop while turning it on. A few video files showed up.

"Look at the last two on the right." She stayed behind the chair and pointed at the screen.

He clicked on the first one, and it brought a street scene from a security camera. The light was not good, but a jogger could be seen leaving a high-rise building. Then a black suburban followed in the same direction at low speed.

"What is this?" Matt had a puzzled look.

"Do you recognize the jogger or the building he's coming from?" She leaned forward.

Matt was trying to focus on the screen, but the soft and warm touch of her bosom on his shoulder plus the feeling of her soft and sweet-scented skin so close to his face made it difficult. Please, d*on't do this to me, Rachel.*

"*Matt*, did you hear me*?*" Rachel turned to face him, and when he looked at her, their faces were almost touching.

He couldn't withstand having such a beautiful woman so close and kissed her on the lips. Rachel engaged in the kissing but then took a step back.

"This doesn't seem right. You have a girlfriend." Her face showed a mixture of dazed desire and amazement.

"Sorry. I couldn't resist. You look gorgeous, and your proximity made me forget everything."

"But you're with Jessica, and she's a great woman."

"Yes, she is, but we had a big argument, and I'm not sure we like the same things." His gaze went toward the window, looking for answers in the sprinkle of white clouds embellishing the clear blue sky.

Rachel put a hand on his shoulder. "Why don't we let this moment pass and focus on the videos? I'm baffled by what just happened and believe we need a break, thinking about something else. We can have a glass of wine on the balcony and talk about your feelings later." Her hand gave his arm a little squeeze.

"You're right. Let's get to work now." He looked again at the video. "That's *Brian.* It's rather dark, but I recognize his hat and running gear plus the front of his building."

"*Great.* I wasn't sure who the jogger was since I never met Brian but notice how suspicious that Suburban is, going at such a low speed."

"This is a good video," Matt sighed, "but it doesn't prove anything."

"No but look at the second video."

This time the video registered a scene from a camera placed across the street from the park. The jogger went by, and the Suburban still followed at low speed. Then there was a moment with no images followed by what seemed to be a homeless person pushing a shopping cart going in the opposite direction.

"I still see Brian jogging and the black Suburban following him."

"Exactly. They were following him because that camera is about five hundred feet from the first one, and there is no way a car would still be behind the jogger unless they were after him. Nobody takes a slow drive through the park before dawn." She pointed again at the screen. "Look at the last part of the scene."

"The homeless person pushing the cart? What does it have to do with the accident?"

"Rewind and look again. We can assume it's a man, but it could be a woman wearing that shabby raincoat. You'll notice that the homeless individual is walking rather fast and looking over their shoulder."

"Yeah, I can see it now. Why is that important?"

"First, he's going in the opposite direction, which means that Brian and the car went by this individual a moment before it was caught on camera. Second, this person is walking fast, and usually, homeless people aren't in a hurry to get anywhere. Third, he is looking over his shoulder. It could indicate he's a little scared of something he saw."

Matt opened his mouth and hit his forehead with his hand. "Wow. You're a *genius.*" He stood up and hugged her.

She gently pushed him back. "Let's not get confused again," and grinned, "for the time being."

"You're right." He took a step back with his palms up. "How did you get those videos?"

"From two merchants who voluntarily provided them when I mentioned I was running an investigation, and by the way, my report would include shots of their shops on TV." She giggled. "Otherwise, trying to get a copy of surveillance cameras would be difficult since it requires an order from a judge. The police wouldn't release the videos. The people we're dealing with seem to have good connections and would obstruct it."

"So, what do we do now? The videos aren't going to be taken as proof of anything in court."

"We need a witness and will need to find that homeless person."

"How? There are hundreds of homeless people in town." He ran his hands through his hair.

"The station has done several reports on homeless people, and they tend to stay in the same place every night, so we may be lucky and find him or her close to the spot where Brian had the accident. I did a preliminary investigation and found a few commercial buildings with porticos in that area that could fit what homeless usually look for to spend the night."

"You've done a remarkable job."

She twirled her hair. "And I hope we can take the next step together."

"You say it and we'll do it."

"Can we get together tomorrow night to drive through that area and see whether we can find our witness? Sunday nights are quiet around there. I wouldn't be surprised if we find this person, but we need to act fast."

"Why wait till night?"

"During the day, homeless people typically walk to shelters, looking for food, a place with bathrooms, or go somewhere they can panhandle, but at night they go back to their favorite spots."

He stood up. "Okay."

"Are you in a hurry?" Rachel tilted her head and got closer.

"Not really."

"Then, why don't we enjoy the sunset on the balcony with a glass of wine? You could share what's bothering you if you want."

"That sounds great. Can I help by opening a bottle?"

"Sure." She pointed to a bar cabinet. "There are a couple of bottles over there. Pick what you want, and I'll bring the glasses to the balcony."

Matt selected a pinot noir and was enjoying the view when she came back. Her ponytail was gone now, and her black hair bounced as she walked from inside, dancing to the rhythm of a song she was humming.

"I brought some cheese and crackers." She poured the wine.

He raised his glass. "To a successful search tomorrow."

"To the beauty of this view and the good company." Rachel's eyes beamed.

He nodded in approval, but his forced smile biting his lip betrayed him.

"Maybe you can share now what's bothering you?"

Matt looked at her wide-open blue eyes and then looked at the sunset. "I had a big argument with Jessica today," Matt said in a shaky voice.

"Don't worry. Those things happen in a relationship, and we both know Jessica loves you. Didn't you see how she was taking care of you at the hospital?"

"Yes, but that's the problem. Jessica worries a lot and is always afraid of something bad happening.

She can't understand that I like to fight for the things I care about, such as protecting the environment. She thinks I should just focus on teaching." Matt shook his head.

Rachel rubbed his back. "You should explain that you love to be involved in social activism like you're doing with the PNA, and sometimes it brings risks. My job is similar, and I understand how you feel."

Matt looked at her. "You're a good friend, and we don't need to keep talking about my problems. How about remembering some of the good old times from our teen years?"

She smiled. They shared and laughed about past stories while the first shadows of the night began to cover the city, and lights glittered everywhere. After a couple of hours, he stood up and moved indoors.

"I'm afraid it's time for me to go. I've had a wonderful time, and you changed my day. Thanks." Matt held her hands while keeping a steady look into her eyes.

"You know you can count on me for whatever you need." She landed a soft kiss on his cheek and hugged him.

Matt put his arms around her and, for an instant, felt that their bodies were a perfect match. His heart was pounding in his chest, and his cheeks were flushing. He took Rachel softly by her bare waist and gently pushed them apart. "I better go before something happens." Then he opened the door to leave.

She wet her lips and winked. "As you wish, but you know where I live." Then pointing a finger, she added, "Remember that we have something important to do tomorrow."

He nodded. "I'll pick you up at eight, and we'll go after that witness."

Rachel closed the door and pumped up her fist. *Yeah.* Then she picked up the phone.

"Tyler, it's Rachel."

"What's up?"

"I don't think we'll need to look further to break up Matt and Jessica's relationship. He told me that they'd had a heated argument and things aren't going well."

"Oh, I've talked to Mary Dalton, and she still doesn't see Matt as a good candidate for her daughter. She's pretending to accept him just to avoid further conflict but is ready to help."

"How?"

"She already planned to have her friend's daughter, who goes to Matt's school, to accuse him of harassment."

"Wow. She *really* dislikes him."

"Yes. And is waiting for us to tell her when to proceed."

"Tell her to put in on hold, but there is something else she can do."

"What's that?"

"She needs to invite Jessica and Matt for dinner tomorrow night. It must sound like it's important."

"You're losing me."

"Tomorrow night, I'm going with Matt to see if we can find a witness who might help prove that his friend Brian didn't die in an accident."

"How's that?"

"I did some research on some surveillance videos, and there's a chance a homeless person may have seen the entire incident. But that's another story."

"So, you want Matt to say that he can't go and further antagonize Jessica."

"*Bingo.* You can share this with Mrs. Dalton so she understands how important it is that Jessica believes that she must go to that dinner and bring Matt with her. She also needs to emphasize how dangerous it is for Matt to keep snooping."

"You're the devil. I'll call her right now." Tyler hung up, grinning.

Chapter 22

MATT COULDN'T SLEEP well. The discussion with Jessica, the prospect of finding a witness to prove Brian's death wasn't an accident, and what had happened at Rachel's apartment were images fighting in his brain. He got up early, poured a cup of coffee, and went out jogging. When he was opening the door of his apartment, the phone rang.

He swallowed, not knowing what to expect. "Hi, Jessica."

"Have you gone running?" Her dry voice made it sound like a mere formality with no interest in what he did.

"Yes. I just came back. How are you today? I think we should talk."

"Agreed. But I have an invitation. My mother called, and they would like to have us for dinner tonight. She says it's important and would like to see both of us."

"Tonight?" He hesitated. "I'm sorry, but I can't make it."

"Why?"

"There's an opportunity to find the witness to Brian's hit-and-run, and the best chance is at night. We can't waste any time. I'm sorry. I hope your parents understand."

"Do you understand how dangerous this is? First, you find a possible link between the brewery fire and some sort of illegal drug trafficking. Now you want to chase those drug mafia guys because you think they may have caused Brian's death? It's *insane*."

"It may sound like that, but I need to know how Brian died."

"How did you find about this potential witness?"

"Rachel did a great job—"

"Rachel?" she interrupted, raising her voice.

"Yes. She's been a big help." Matt explained how she had found the videos and the urgency in the follow-up.

"Can't she go look for that witness so you can be at my parent's house tonight?"

"We are both going to look for the witness."

She couldn't hide her irritation. "Oh, *how convenient.*"

"It's not what you think." A tense silence followed. "We don't really know whether this is a man or a woman. If it's a woman, she would be more comfortable talking to another woman, and if it's a man, which we think it is, then we don't want to have Rachel by herself. Josh went to visit his parents, so I have to be there."

"That's considerate on your part. You have to protect Rachel."

"Don't be sarcastic."

"Josh can visit his parents, but you can't have dinner with mine." Her anger was loud and clear. "You do whatever you want. I'll be at my parents' house for dinner and hope to see you there." Jessica hung up.

TYLER CALLED HIS father. "Dad, there's something important you should know about Matt and his friends."

"What is he up to now?"

"They're looking for a witness who may prove that his friend, Brian's, death was not an accident." Tyler shared what he had heard from Rachel but couldn't see his father shaking his fist with impotence.

"Thanks, Tyler. Call me anytime you get new information."

They hung up, and Frank leaned back in his chair, looking at the ceiling. *This is getting out of control.* He stood up, went to the window, looking for an answer, and decided to alert his partners.

THE DAY WENT by, and Jessica was a nervous wreck. She tried to keep her mind busy by cleaning the apartment she had moved into, baking some cookies, and doing some online shopping, but by mid-afternoon, she couldn't take it anymore and decided to go to her parents' house. When Jessica arrived, the maid opened the door and a voice from inside asked, "Who is it?" but before she could answer, Mary came to the foyer.

She hugged her daughter. "*Jessica*, I didn't expect you so early."

"I finished all I had to do and thought it would be nice to spend more time with you and Daddy."

Mary noticed her tight-lipped smile and hesitation. "Is there anything wrong? Come in and tell us what's going on."

They went into the family room where John was reading. A three-piece chaise sectional in black leather and two ivory accent chairs surrounding a Persian carpet with gold and purple motives next to a fireplace reminded Jessica of happy family moments.

"Hi, Jessica." His father's smile was comforting. "Where's Matt?"

She blushed. *I better talk to them now.* "I'm not sure whether he'll be joining us."

John raised his eyebrows while Mary rolled her eyes. "Why wouldn't he come?"

Jessica looked down and mumbled. "It's a long story."

"Then come and sit. We're here to help. Tell us what's going on." Mary took her daughter's hands.

She mentioned the discussions with Matt over the last couple of days and the search for the witness that same evening.

"Those may be some short-term disagreements. All couples fight and then talk it over to solve the problems." John tried to be supportive.

"I don't think so," Jessica shook her head. "This is about what he likes to do regardless of how I feel about it." Tears began rolling from her eyes in advance of the tsunami of contained feelings that followed while her head rested on her mother's shoulder.

"That's okay, darling. Let it go." Mary held her daughter by the shoulders while stroking her hair. "Julie, bring some tea and water."

They kept comforting her until she calmed down.

"Sorry to bring my worries to you." Jessica was still sobbing.

"We understand. You're going through a rough time, and it's not easy to accept disappointment from someone we love. It looks like Matt gets carried away by pursuing his objectives no matter the consequences. Do you think there's anything valid in the obsession with the brewery? Maybe the skiing incident was an accident after all and, if it wasn't, he didn't learn he's in danger." Mary was following the line of thought suggested by Tyler.

"I'm afraid that I may agree with your mother this time." John steepled his fingers. "His fixation on solving this without letting the police do their job, if there is anything to investigate, doesn't make sense. And he's running a high risk. Knowing how worried you are, he should be more considerate of your feelings. He's acting too independently and recklessly, and that's not good for someone building a long-term relationship."

Jessica squirmed in her chair. "What should I do?"

Mary looked at her straight in the eyes. "I believe you should make it clear that it's time for him to make a choice. Either he gives the police the information about the suspicions he has, or the relationship doesn't work with him running around and risking his and your lives."

John nodded in approval.

MATT PICKED UP Rachel at her apartment and drove to the area where Brian had lived and had had the accident. She pointed to the stores that had agreed to share the videos to give him a perspective of the location. The night was cold, and they slowly drove along the park line about eight hundred yards in both directions from the point of the hit-and-run. They made two passes without any results.

"Do you think he will be around here tonight?" Matt's lips curled in disbelief.

"We have to be patient. Let's do a couple of more turns. This area is dark, and homeless people don't want to be seen." Rachel's eyes were scanning the buildings.

They were back close to the spot of the accident.

"*Look.*" Rachel pointed to a bench a few yards inside the park. "I think someone is coming from that area. Stop, and let's watch."

A blurred shadow from the darkness of the park was approaching the sidewalk. The figure was walking slowly and looked in both directions of the street.

They parked and got closer, being careful not to be seen. "It seems to be a man."

Matt was hyperventilating. "And he has a shopping cart. The coat and hat look like those in the videos."

The mysterious man crossed the street and went to a covered alley of a furniture store. He took a blanket from the cart, put it on the concrete, lay down, and was ready to cover himself with a coat when Matt and Rachel got next to him.

"What are you looking at? Are you police?" he barked. His peppered beard, long hair, and wrinkles showed signs of prolonged exposure to the weather, but his vivid eyes had the intensity of someone not as old as he looked. He was probably in his early fifties but appeared to be in his mid-sixties.

"No. Calm down. We just want to ask you a few questions." Rachel extended her arms with her palms down, trying to be as reassuring as possible.

"Questions?" He frowned.

Matt decided to appeal to the guy's feelings. "My name is Matt. Two months ago, early on a Sunday, my best friend, Brian, was hit by a car right here, and the driver ran away without helping him. He later died in the hospital, and we're trying to find who did it."

The man's quizzical look invited Matt to continue.

"His younger sister's life has been destroyed. We don't want to cause any trouble, but we have reason to believe that you may have seen the accident."

"How so?"

"Because we've been able to get a couple of videos from shop owners in the neighborhood who want to help us." Rachel took her phone from her purse and showed the man the videos. "There's not a lot of light, but we recognize you by your hat, coat, and the cart. And you seem to be looking backward in the direction of the accident."

He shook his head. "I don't want to be in any trouble."

"You won't be. I promise. We just want to confirm whether the car hit my friend on purpose. Please."

He scratched his head. "Who would believe a hobo?"

"We will." Matt stared at him.

An endless minute followed until the man stood up. "You seem to care about your friend, and I wish I had friends like you." He was looking down and then peered up at Matt. "I always get up early because the guard of this shop allows me to sleep here but only when it's dark outside, and I hide behind this pillar, but I have to leave before anybody comes to the shop and can see me. A question of image, he told me, and it's a good arrangement since this is a protected spot from rain and cold to spend the night."

Matt was shifting his weight from one foot to the other with clenched fists behind his back, waiting for the man to get to the point.

"That morning, I was crouched down behind the pillar to gather my things when I saw the black car following the jogger and then accelerate, bumping and lifting him into the air."

Rachel put her hands over her mouth, gasping.

"Do you think it was an accident? Did my friend get in front of the car somehow?" Matt's questions were coming fast.

"That was no accident. The car sped up and hit the man, leaving at high speed. I picked up my stuff as fast as I could and walked away. When I was about two hundred yards away, I noticed someone getting closer to the body, and in a few minutes, a patrol car flew by me toward the spot of the accident. Your video shows the moment I was trying to get out and looking back at them."

"*I knew it. I knew it.*" Matt hit the pillar with his fist. "Thank you for telling us."

"Would you be willing to repeat it in a video?" Rachel noticed the man's reluctance and quickly added. "I'm Rachel Avila from Channel 5 and can shoot a video blurring your face so nobody would know it's you."

"I've already told you what I saw. What would I get by sharing this on camera and running the risk of someone recognizing me?"

"What do you need? If you want some sort of compensation, I'm sure my news director would do something."

"Pay me? Why people always think that giving some money solves the homeless problems?" He pointed a finger. "Because everybody thinks that hobos are lazy, always drunk, don't want to work and that's why they are on the streets?" Now he was raising his voice. "There might some that fit that image, but I had a heart operation and was in a hospital for two months. The bills and prescriptions drained my savings, but I had a good job as a floor supervisor in an appliances store. Luck turned against me one month later when the company I was working for shut down. I moved to a single room rental but couldn't afford that either because it's not easy to find a job in your fifties, so I ended up here." His shallow, rapid breathing and wide-open eyes scared Rachel. "Do you know what I want?" He got closer to her, and Matt moved in between them. "I want a job. If you can get me that, I'll do your bloody video."

Rachel quickly put herself back together. "I can help you. I'll make a report of your situation, and we'll tell your story on TV. I'm convinced that it will get someone to offer you a job. Of course, that's if you're okay with it."

"You get me a job, lady, and I'll tell everybody about that SOB who hit your friend." He grinned.

"Okay. Tomorrow I'll come back and meet you at the park across the street at four in the afternoon. I'll bring the camera and put together your story."

Then Matt added, "Do you need some money to spend the night in a hotel?"

"Appreciate your offer, but if I leave this premium spot, I'll lose it to another homeless person. It's tough to keep a good place. I'll be fine."

"Thank you. You didn't tell us your name."

"Call me Jimmy. Now, if you'll excuse me, I need to get some sleep."

NOBODY NOTICED A red SUV driving by. When Matt and Rachel were close to his car, they heard the shot and instinctively turned around to see the SUV speeding away and leaving skid marks on the pavement.

"*Jimmy,*" Rachel cried out in shock while Matt ran back to the spot where they had left him.

"*Call an ambulance,*" he shouted at the sight of the homeless man's body lying on the blanket with a red stream coming out from his chest.

Matt and Rachel were still trying to recover from the turmoil they had just gone through when the siren of a patrol car arriving brought them back.

"Did you place an emergency call?" a heavyset policeman asked.

"Yes, Officer. A man was shot."

The officers blocked the perimeter of the scene and scanned the area.

A few minutes later, an ambulance showed up. The paramedics gave the homeless person some oxygen, quickly put him on a stretcher and were ready to go when Rachel approached them.

"How is he?" Rachel's hands were still shaking.

"Still alive but don't know whether he'll make it. It's a serious wound. We'll take him to the hospital right now."

THE POLICE OFFICER approached them. "Do you know the victim?" Rachel was going to answer, but Matt's stare froze her. "No. We just happened to be coming back to our car from the park when we heard the shot, saw a red SUV speeding away, and called 9-1-1," Matt replied with a firm voice.

"You can leave then. Just give us your contact information in case we need to talk to you. We'll go through the victim's belongings to look for an ID or some clue of his activities and then clear the area."

"What do you think happened?" Matt unconsciously raised his voice.

"It could have been a fight between homeless people for this spot, but that's not probable because they usually fight with their fists, bats, or sometimes knifes. It looks more like a drive-by shooting related to gangs settling a difference or a drug-related crime."

"Officer, I'm Rachel Avila from Channel 5 and have been covering stories about homeless people. I want to learn more about the case after you do the investigation."

"You can find me at the police station, Precinct 23."

Matt and Rachel looked at the red and white dazzling lights of the ambulance gleaning in the night, wondering how all happened so quickly. They didn't talk for a few minutes and then got into Matt's car.

Rachel looked at him. "Why did you say that we didn't know Jimmy?"

"Because the situation was confusing, and he's a key witness. What if the same people who went after Brian are involved in this one also? I don't trust everybody on the police force and don't want them to know that we've already talked to Jimmy."

"What if Jimmy talks to the police and tells them about our conversation?"

"You heard the paramedic. He may not survive. We run the risk and figure out what to say if needed later."

Chapter 23

O N THE WAY back to Rachel's apartment, her cell phone rang.

"Ms. Avila, this is Sheriff White. Excuse me for calling so late, but I thought you would like to know that we found the two skiers who harassed Matt."

Rachel looked at Matt, smiling. "That's wonderful."

"They were in a small Texas town and were arrested for DUI. The local police checked the records and found that we were looking for them, so they are being questioned right now about the skiing incident."

"Thanks, Sheriff. Let me know what you find out."

"What's that excitement about?" Matt glanced at her, and she shared the good news.

"*Fantastic.*" He raised a fist. "This time, we'll get them. We have those two guys who threatened me,

Jimmy's videos, and evidence on the material used in illegal drug production." Then he looked at Rachel. "We need to share all this information with the sheriff. I don't trust the local police being impartial to DB Corp., and he'll surely tell us what to do. Can you arrange to meet him asap?"

"Definitely. It is a great story." Her journalist side couldn't hide the eagerness to land a successful news alert hit on prime time.

They arrived at Rachel's apartment, and she invited him to come in for a cup of coffee, but he gently refused. First, *I need to clear out my feelings.* Matt went home.

"Tyler? This is Rachel. Thought it would be good to share my progress." She described the meeting with the hobo and the call from Sheriff White. "Matt is more determined than ever to keep pursuing the case against DB Corp., and it won't be good news for Jessica. Have you heard anything from her mother?"

"Good news also. Jessica is angry at Matt because she feels ignored, and his attention is always focused on the investigations, no matter the risks. Her mother told her to think about whether that was the relationship she wanted, and surprisingly, her father supported her mother's advice. That's good news because Jessica trusts her father's advice."

"Great. Let's keep in touch. Matt wants to set up a meeting with Sheriff White tomorrow to share all the information and move forward against DB Corp. He thinks the brewery operation is hiding some sort of drug trafficking or manufacturing and wants to get a warrant to inspect their facilities."

"Wow. That sounds big." *It sounds like Matt will get in more trouble with Jessica.* Tyler was salivating.

"DAD, I HAVE some news for you about Matt."

"What this time, Tyler?" Frank began to fidget on his chair.

Tyler shared what he had learned about the potential witness, the capture of the two suspects in Matt's ski accident, and the intention to get a warrant to inspect the brewery facilities.

After thanking his son for the information, Frank picked up the phone. "Don, how much time do you need to implement the emergency plan?" he snapped.

"Frank? Why don't you calm down and tell me more?"

The lawyer raised his voice. "There is no time to calm down. You may receive a search warrant for the brewery as early as tomorrow."

"Why?" Don Backman froze.

"That guy, Matt, found out about some materials used in the lab and put it together with the threat he received by your two guys to guess that the brewery operation is hiding something and is going to the police."

"But we can control that. Can't we?"

"We have good contacts but not with everyone at the police department. I can buy some time, but you tell me how long it will take to execute the plan."

"We've done it before when we knew inspections were coming. We'll need seventy-two hours."

"Okay. I'll work through my contacts to make sure you have that time before the police show up. Also, do the captured guys know what to say?"

"Don't worry. They received the instructions you suggested."

"Good. Let's get to work."

MATT GOT TOGETHER with Josh for lunch the next day and updated him on his progress with Rachel's help.

Josh grinned. "It looks like everything is getting better."

"Not everything." Matt played with his food.

"Not all is solved, but we've come a long way in the investigation."

"The investigation is running great, but…"

Josh leaned forward as he noticed his friend's flushing face. "What's wrong?"

"It's Jessica. Our relationship is going downhill fast."

"*What*? You seemed to be happy with each other."

"She's worried about my involvement with the DB Corp. case and the search for whoever was responsible for Brian's death. She suffered through my recovery after the skiing incident and is concerned that what happened to Brian may happen to me if I continue searching. When she learned about the possible illegal drug operation at the brewery, her patience went over the limit. We've had some serious arguments."

"Maybe she'll cool down and understand."

"I don't think so." Matt looked away. "I didn't go to an important dinner at her parents' house last night because I was trying to identify a potential witness to Brian's murder."

"And she knew about the conflict?"

"Yes, and for her, it was another example of being neglected once more."

Josh tilted his head. "Maybe she's right. You did that right after she complained about not receiving your attention? Not a good move. Why didn't you call me? I could've gone with Rachel."

"That's what she said. And there's more. She may be jealous of Rachel."

Josh blew out the cheeks and exhaled. "And does she have any reason to be?"

"Not sure. Jessica's always so worried and not

supporting me." He paused. "On the other hand, Rachel is so full of energy and willing to take risks."

"My friend, we both know Jessica is a wonderful woman, and you've had something serious going on for some time. Rachel is beautiful, and you have good memories from high school but don't know much about who she is now."

"You're right, but I'm confused."

"I understand, but I think you need to have a long conversation with Jessica and figure out where the relationship is. She deserves that."

Matt rolled his eyes. "Enough about this. Let's talk about what we have to do next."

"Can't you see, Matt? She may be right in that you're obsessed with the DB Corp. investigation."

Matt shook his head in denial and ignored the comment. "Rachel is going to set up a meeting with Sheriff White to share the information we have. Hopefully, he can tell us about what the police got from questioning those thugs who threatened me."

Matt called Rachel after finishing his day teaching.

"Matt? Did you get my message? I talked to Sheriff White, and he expects us at his office in Crystal County tomorrow at ten. He was excited about the information I shared and is going to analyze the videos. He's also going to contact a friend he has at the DEA to learn more about those materials found at the site of the lab fire."

"Wonderful. I'll take the day off."

"There's more but not so good news. I got a call from the cop who met us at the site of Jimmy's shooting."

"What does he want?"

"He did some investigation. The police checked the street cameras that show a red SUV. They want us to identify the vehicle, and he also has questions about Jimmy."

"Did he talk?" Matt froze.

"He's barely conscious but mumbled something about a man and a woman talking to him, and the police want to go with us to the hospital to determine whether Jimmy recognizes us. What are we going to do?" Rachel grabbed her phone nervously.

"Let's not panic. We'll see what happens."

"You're right. We can always deny what Jimmy says. If he recognizes us, we can argue that he has probably seen me on TV and he's confused."

"That's right. I'll see you at the police station later." Matt exhaled and hung up.

I don't know what I would do without Rachel. She's such a trooper. At that moment, his phone rang.

"Jessica, I was going to call you. Sorry, I couldn't make it last night."

"Did you get what you were looking for?" The

sarcasm in her voice didn't hide the dryness of her tone.

"We found a witness who says it was not an accident."

"And you'll continue to look into it, of course."

"I have to."

"Look, we have to talk. This situation can't continue. Can we get together for dinner?"

This is going to be bad. "I can't tonight."

"Why?"

"Someone shot the witness, and we have to go to the police station to make some vehicle identifications. I don't know how long it will take, but it's important." He braced for the reply biting his lip.

"Then breakfast tomorrow?"

Matt stumbled with his words. "Can't then, either." He looked up as if searching for divine inspiration. "We have to be at the sheriff's office in Crystal County at ten, so we'll have to leave early."

"Well," her words felt like daggers in his ears, "maybe there's no need to talk then. You're confirming my assumptions. If you can't ever find time for me, it means you don't care about our relationship."

He tried a weak defense. "But I still love you."

That was like throwing gasoline onto a fire. "You turned out to be a cheat and a hypocrite." She raised her voice. "Go play detective with your little friend but never talk to me again."

The line went dead and left Matt with a frozen look at his cell phone, talking to himself. *Matt, you've done it. You just threw away a wonderful relationship of two years with an amazing woman.* He decided to walk to his apartment, looking for answers in the cool breeze of a lovely afternoon.

A couple of hours later, Matt and Rachel went to the police station.

"Good afternoon, Officer. We understand you want us to identify the vehicle we saw at the scene of the accident?" Matt pretended to be calm.

"Yes. Let's look at a couple of videos from the street cameras." The officer stood up and guided them to a small room where Matt and Rachel confirmed it was the same red SUV they had seen the night before."

"Good," the officer smiled, "we have some shots that show the license plate so we may be able to identify the owner." Then he kept his gaze on both of them. "Now, I would like to go to the hospital to check with the victim. He seems to remember talking to a man and a woman before the shooting. You mentioned that you didn't know him, but did you exchange any words?"

"We'll be happy to cooperate. The man may have waved at us, but we don't know him." Rachel was opening a way out of their lie.

A patrol car took them to the hospital, and the officer went straight to the ICU, where a colleague was on duty to protect the victim. When they arrived, a doctor was coming out of the ICU.

"Officer, if you're here to see the victim of the shooting, I hate to say that, unfortunately, he just died a few minutes ago."

Matt and Rachel exchanged a look of relief while the officer observed them.

"Well, it seems there is nothing else to do here. You can go now, and I'll let you know if there is any progress in this case. I'm afraid the only thing we have is a license plate number. We know it belongs to a rental car picked up at the airport by two Mexican nationals."

Chapter 24

J OSH SAT NEXT to a window at Café Paris, looking at the passing pedestrians while conflicting thoughts were racing through his mind. A soft knock on the window brought his attention back. There she was, wearing a dark-blue pantsuit with a white shirt and a discrete gold chain. The relaxed curls of her blond hair allowed her green eyes' luminescence to highlight her face's delicate features. *She's beautiful.* He waved, and she joined at the table after greeting him with a kiss on the cheek.

"Josh, thanks for accepting my invitation to have breakfast this morning." She tried to control the quiver of her voice.

He stared into her eyes. "You know you can count on me, Jessica. The sound of your voice last night was so sad that I felt I had to be here. Besides, Matt told me about the issues in your relationship."

"I feel I can trust you. I already talked with my

parents about it but, since you know Matt very well, I want to have your thoughts, too."

"Sure. Can you share what's bothering you?" He gave her a reassuring smile. "But first, let's order something. Talking on an empty stomach is not good."

They ordered the famous Café Paris croissants while chatting about the place and the weather. After the waiter brought their order, he took her hand.

"Feeling a little better now?"

"Yes," she said with a half-smile on her face. "Things are not going well with Matt. The last few times we've talked, we just argued because I feel like I'm not important to him anymore." Her fingers were nervously playing with the sugar packets.

"Why is that?"

"It seems like all he cares about lately is the brewery investigation. I warned him that it could be dangerous, and I suffer a lot, but he wouldn't listen."

"I see how this affects you, but we found some incriminating information that makes it exciting."

"But to the point of not having time for me? A couple of nights ago, he missed a dinner invitation from my parents that was important to them. I told him that we need to talk, and he never has time. First, he went with Rachel to find a witness. Last night couldn't have dinner with me because they had to go to the police station since someone shot the witness. I also suggested having breakfast today, but he went to Crystal County with Rachel *again.*" Her eyes narrowed.

"I told him that I could have gone with Rachel to look for the witness on Sunday, but they didn't call me." He opened his hands.

"I know. I asked Matt why not let you go since we needed to talk, but he said he didn't want to spoil the visit to your parents."

Josh raised his eyebrows.

"And why did he need to go today? Couldn't you or Rachel handle that?"

"I agreed to go but canceled when you called me."

"You see." She raised her hands. "You're my friend and decided to come to talk with me, but my fiancé can't find the time."

"Rachel, calm down. What did your parents say?"

"You know Matt never was good enough for my mother, but this time, she was fair. She suggested that Matt and I need to discuss the situation and whether his activities and the worries that cause me could damage our relationship in the long term."

"It sounds like good advice."

"And my father agreed. I trust him." Jessica looked straight at his eyes. "May I ask you a question?"

"Of course."

"Is there anything going on between Matt and Rachel?"

Josh scratched his temple and opened his eyes wide. "You're my friend, so I'll share what I sense. The answer is that I don't know. I know he loves you, but I would say that he has been confused lately. He understands that you're worried, but on the other hand, he believes that he should follow through with the investigation. He gets along well with Rachel, and she's also the type of person who doesn't look at consequences. Maybe it is her journalistic instinct."

"I hear you, but I think that love should take precedence over work in a relationship. I wish he would have canceled the trip to Crystal County as you did." She put her hand over his.

"We all have different priorities." He seemed to perceive some sparks in her beautiful green eyes. "What are you going to do?"

"I'm disappointed in Matt and can't continue like this. He's not changing, so it's going to be better to end the relationship and move on with our lives."

"No matter what you decide, know I'm here for whatever you need."

They kept talking, and she mentioned her father's plan to leave the partnership with Frank Morris and open a new practice with her as a partner. That was the important announcement that the Daltons shared with her during dinner at their home.

"My father is not comfortable being associated with Frank anymore."

"And why is that?"

"He feels that his partner has a relationship

with DB Corp. that goes beyond typical services and suspects the firm is overcharging for its legal services."

"Does he think that Frank is cheating on the bills?"

"No, and that's the problem. Why would Frank have such a close relationship with Don Brackman, the head of DB Corp., if he's overcharging for legal services? Anyway, my father feels he doesn't need to know and is breaking apart on good terms with the excuse of becoming independent and allowing me to grow."

"Good move. Sometimes you have to let it go when something doesn't look right."

"I wish Matt would understand that." She pointed out.

He smiled. "Remember that I'm an environmental lawyer. If your father needs one, let me know."

"That's right. I see you as a friend and never think you are a lawyer. It could be a good idea since neither my dad nor I have much experience in environmental litigations."

"I was half-joking, but it would be great to work with you and your father."

The conversation continued increasingly animated until she looked at her watch. "Oh my God. I didn't know it was so late. I have to run." A smile illuminated her face, and she hugged him. "Thanks so much. You've changed my day."

"Glad to hear that, Jessica. You deserve to be happy." He saw her leaving the café and shook his head. *Matt is a dumbass. How can he risk losing someone like Jessica?*

SHERIFF WHITE WAS at his office when Matt and Rachel arrived. He invited them to move to a small conference room that had a table and three chairs. The austere setting made Matt feel like someone was watching from behind glass, like in the movies. There was a projector in the middle of the table connected to a laptop the sheriff turned on.

"Thanks for coming. I've reviewed the videos you sent me and want to show you something." Sheriff White proceeded without preambles as he usually did and pointed to the screen. "Let's look first at the videos from your friend's accident. We've enhanced the view and can see a license plate on the black vehicle." The screen showed a light-blue-color license plate with a darker blue stripe at the bottom and the characters A56-47-05.

"It looks like an out-of-state license?" Matt frowned.

"If you look carefully at the bottom, there are some words partially covered with mud that seem to say Baja California. We checked the color and format, and it matches the license plates issued in Tijuana. It's a vehicle that came from Mexico."

"Some sicarios from across the border?" Rachel's eyes were wide open.

"Or a driver from Mexico afraid of what was going to happen if found guilty and fled from the scene."

"And how about the second video with the hobo looking back at the accident like he was trying to escape?" Matt insisted.

"Or just being curious about what happened. It's natural to look back if you hear the noise of someone hit by a car."

"But we talked to that person, and he confirmed that it was not an accident." Matt sat back in the chair and crossed his arms.

"And where is that witness?"

"He was shot and killed after talking to us."

"I see."

"I know that it may sound strange, but we're telling you what we found out." Rachel saw a shadow of doubt on the sheriff's face.

"Okay. Let me tell you about the two guys arrested in Texas who were involved in your accident. The local police interrogated them, and they admitted to skiing at Crystal Mountain on that weekend."

Matt leaned forward, eager to hear some good news.

"However, they said they saw you earlier in the day having a physical confrontation with another guy. Is that true?"

"Yes, but it had nothing to do with them," Matt mumbled.

"They mentioned you were in the gondola going up the mountain looking sad and not saying a word. Their statement indicated that you took long turns across the trail's width when you began going down the mountain. They were worried about your safety since they thought you were depressed. At that time, they got closer to ask whether everything was okay but left when you told them all was fine."

"Those are lies." Matt raised his voice.

"But it's consistent with the statement made by Tyler Morris, who said he saw you and those individuals skiing together, like friends. Now we have two statements made by people not related to each other who could support the notion that you had an accident not caused by the actions of anyone else."

Matt shook his head, and Rachel intervened. "Sheriff, how about if those two guys are lying?"

"It's a possibility," Sheriff White said while looking at both in the eyes. "But you have to understand that we have a weak case. The alleged threats to Matt and his friend's death in retaliation for investigating too far into DB Corp.'s activities are not based on strong evidence. It could be presented as a baseless conspiracy theory. That could expose you to a big lawsuit by the corporation. Are you sure you want to continue with this?"

Matt stood up. "Sheriff, I received threats on the mountain, and we talked to the witness of Brian's hit-and-run. We also saw how someone shot the witness. There is no way that this is just our imagination." He planted his hands on the table and leaned forward.

The sheriff pinched the bridge of his nose and closed his eyes for a few seconds. "Very well. I told Ms. Avila the first time I met her that I suspect DB Corp. had used some influences to cover up something in the past but suggesting that they may want to hurt people seems to go a little too far. Anyway, what you have is not enough to convince a judge to issue a search warrant to look for illegal substances at their facilities."

Matt threw his hand up in the air while pacing the room. "Here we go again. No basis for a thorough investigation like fifteen years ago."

"However," Sheriff White continued, "the only opportunity we have is to get the interest of the DEA. Based on suspect illegal drug manufacturing activities, they can build a case for an inspection warrant based on a possible federal crime."

"Let's talk to them." Matt quickly turned his head to face the sheriff.

"I've talked to someone I know, and he's interested in talking to you. They've been investigating this area for many years because they suspect there's a lab producing amphetamines and other drugs."

"Have they thought that the brewery has something to do with it?"

"No. Sometimes the authorities detect clandestine

operations by looking into unusual electricity and water consumption. A large brewery consumes a lot of electricity and more than ten gallons of water per gallon of beer. Also, there is a lot of traffic receiving supplies and distributing beer, so it would be a great place to hide an illegal operation. He said it's unusual because responsible large corporations usually own breweries subject to OSHA and other inspections. However, it may be worth checking out. He's arriving tonight and expects to see you sometime this week."

"Thanks for your help, Sheriff."

"I'll give you the benefit of the doubt on your story but still think it's a weak case unless the DEA decides it's worth pursuing. Get in contact with their agent."

Chapter 25

A COUPLE OF DAYS later, John was packing his belongings at the office when Frank came in. "John, I still don't understand why you want to leave our firm and become independent. We've had a great partnership for several years."

"That's right, Frank, but I believe it's time for me to work with Jessica and help her grow something that will become hers in the future."

Frank looked at him, reclined on the door frame. *He sounds sincere and doesn't look like he suspects anything.* "As you wish, but you know we can still collaborate on cases."

"I intend to work with the clients I've been serving if they want to continue with me and let you keep yours." John kept packing.

"Of course, just send me a list to make sure we don't overlap and confuse them. I hope that our families will keep in touch."

"Frank, this is just a break in our partnership. Nothing personal." John smirked.

When Frank left, Jessica came in. "What does he want?"

"Nothing, I guess checking on why we're leaving the firm."

"Did you mention anything about your reservations regarding DB Corp. and his close relationship to Don Brackman?"

"No, I want to leave it clear that DB Corp. is his client, and he always dealt personally with the president. All the minutes from all the meetings reflect it. I don't need to worry in case there is something obscure. I also documented my recent questioning of the large amounts billed to DB Corp. for services I didn't remember the firm providing."

"You're right. We better leave this place as soon as possible and start our own business. By the way, do you think we can add an environmental lawyer?"

"That seems to be a great idea. It's a growing field, and we don't have a lot of expertise in the area. We'll look for someone."

"No need to look, Dad." She smiled, and her eyes were glittering.

"I see that you're one step ahead. Who's that person?"

"Josh Miller."

"Your sweetheart from high school and Matt's friend? I didn't know he's a lawyer."

"He is and will be happy to join us if you approve it."

"Tell him to come by the house this afternoon. Seeing your excitement, I can't think of a reason why we shouldn't talk to him."

Jessica hugged her father. "I'll call him."

BEFORE GOING TO Lakeview, Matt met with Josh over a cup of coffee to share the results of the meeting with Sheriff White. He described how uncomfortable he felt with the sheriff's questions.

"It seemed like he didn't believe those guys caused the skiing incident since they told the police a fabricated story, and he even showed doubts about our conversation with the witness of Brian's accident."

Josh leaned back. "Maybe because he's used to challenging everything, especially when there are conflicting statements."

"Anyway," Matt raised his palm, "he gave us a contact at the DEA who wants to see us this afternoon. We need to make the case so he agrees to inspect the brewery lab." His eyes were glowing with excitement.

"That's great. But this afternoon? I'm afraid I can't. You and Rachel can take care of it."

"Can't go?" Matt frowned. "C'mon, Josh. This

is the opportunity we've looking for. What's so important that you can't postpone?"

"I have an appointment for a new job."

"I didn't know you were looking."

"I wasn't, but Jessica's father decided to break his partnership and start his own firm with his daughter, and they need an environmental lawyer, so I'm going to their house today for an interview."

Matt tilted his head and tightened his lips. "Working with Jessica?"

"Yes. I hope so. By the way, how is your situation with her?"

"The last time we talked was three days ago, and it was over the phone. Jessica was mad at me for going to Crystal Mountain with Rachel and told me not to call her anymore." Matt looked down while absentmindedly stirring his coffee.

"Why didn't you call her after that?"

"Because the last few times we've talked, she ended up being furious, and it's always because of our investigations."

"Have you tried to take some time to be with her? She asked me whether something is going on between you and Rachel."

He scowled. "When did you talk to her?"

"She called me after your last discussion, but that's not the point. Have you made up your mind regarding your feelings for Jessica and Rachel?"

"I've been with Jessica for more than two years.

She cares for me, but sometimes I feel like she's too controlling. On the other hand, I find that Rachel shares my same interests and is more determined and energetic."

"I believe you need to find an answer because neither one deserves to be played. Both are great women."

"How about you? Do you have any feelings for them?"

Josh raised his eyebrows, surprised by the unexpected question. "Look, we've been close friends for a long time. You know that Jessica was my first love from high school, and I've always liked her. Rachel is gorgeous and intelligent, but if I had a choice, I would prefer Jessica. I've always been respectful of your relationship and wished for it to work well, but if you decide to break it off, I'll try to get closer to her."

Matt looked at him straight in the eyes, not knowing whether to get mad or smile. "I've known of your admiration for Jessica but also appreciate your friendship and openness. You're right. I need to get closure on this."

"Be conscious that you'll need to work hard if you want to rebuild your relationship with Jessica."

"Don't worry, my friend. The way she talked to me last time gave little room for reconciliation, and I'm deeply committed to the investigation, so I believe we have an answer. I'll talk to her to make everything clear."

"So, are you saying that your relationship with Jessica is over?" Josh's eyes brightened.

"And if she likes you, maybe it's the best for everybody."

MATT CALLED JESSICA. "We need to talk. I know you've tried to see me, and I wasn't able to meet, but I believe it's time to discuss in person what's going on with our relationship."

Jessica didn't say a word for a few seconds. "Fine. We'll talk, and the sooner, the better. How about during your lunch break?"

"That's fine. Could you come to the Italian restaurant near the school? That would give us some more time before I go back to class."

She replied with a nervous voice, "I'll see you there at noon."

THEY GOT A table at a corner of the restaurant with relative privacy. After exchanging some vague remarks about the weather and ordering some food, Matt looked at her eyes. "Jessica, I know I've been disappointing you lately, and I apologize for it."

She looked down while playing with the napkin. "Is that all you have to say?"

"No. I've been thinking about my involvement with the investigation and your concerns."

She didn't say anything and looked at him with sad eyes.

Matt felt his heart shrinking for what he was going to say. "Jessica, I love you, but I believe my lifestyle and involvement in social issues and sometimes getting into trouble is not what you expect from a long-term relationship. This is who I am, and I don't want to hurt you. But I'm also not going to change. It's not fair to you or me to ask me to, either."

Now her eyes lightened up with anger. "You're right. I'm not going to stay home, waiting for you to come back from your quixotic quests." Then her tone softened. "The last few days have been illuminating for me also, and I've been thinking, too. I've concluded that this relationship doesn't have a future despite loving you, and it is better to decide that now rather than risking a fall later when we may have a family. I believe you're selfish and unwilling to change, and that's not what I want for a long-term relationship."

Matt looked at her and the tears clouding her beautiful eyes. "I'm sorry, Jess. You deserve something better than me, but I'll be around as a friend if you allow me."

Jessica got up. "Yeah. Maybe friends." And then she left.

RACHEL AND MATT met with the DEA agent and were surprised to see how open he was to listen to the fire story, the hit-and-run, Matt's accident, and the witness's murder.

"Did you say that the vehicle involved in Brian's accident had Tijuana's license plates?"

"Yes, does it tell you anything?"

"It's not unusual for drug cartels to do the dirty job as needed when their operation is compromised."

Matt looked at Rachel and then to the agent. "Are you saying that a Mexican drug cartel could be in the middle of all this? The police told us that a couple of Mexican nationals rented the SUV involved in the witness murder."

"One more reason to believe they could be involved. Cartels look for all sorts of partnerships to get a foothold wherever they can and expand their operations. If there is anything involving illegal drugs, I wouldn't be surprised if one of those cartels is part of it. We've been following the Tijuana cartel and believe they have been operating around here."

"Are you going to inspect the brewery?"

"I'm going to present a petition for a warrant and hopefully get it, but make sure you don't share this with anybody."

"We won't. Please call us if you get it. Matt works as a teacher, but I'm available any time." Rachel wanted to make sure she wouldn't miss the breaking news.

MATT AND RACHEL left the DEA's office thrilled with the news.

"This is cause for celebration. How about dinner? You pick the place." Matt was finally seeing that all his efforts were paying out.

"*Yes.*" Rachel took a couple of quick steps in front of him before turning back and facing Matt. "And I know the perfect place."

"Wonderful. Just tell me, and we go there."

"Dinner at my place. We'll cook together." Her bright smile couldn't receive a negative answer.

Matt grinned. "That's the way it is then. Not sure if you're ready for my cooking, but we'll try." He took her hand and walked toward a taxi.

As soon as they arrived at Rachel's apartment, she pointed him to the bar. "Why don't you prepare some drinks? I'll go and change into something more casual."

He poured a couple of glasses of a Sonoma County Chardonnay and was admiring the view from the balcony when she came from behind.

"Still thinking about the inspection of the brewery lab?" Rachel was wearing black leggings with an orange mesh top over a black bra. He turned around, and his eyes went wide open.

"*Wow.* You look gorgeous. I can't think of the brewery right now."

She moistened her lips, made deep eye contact, and moved closer. "Are you flirting with me?"

He couldn't resist any longer and took her by the waist while landing a soft kiss on her lips.

"Wait." Rachel put her palms on his chest, pushing back slightly. "What are we getting into? You still have Jessica. Are you sure you want to do this?"

He kept his hands on her waist. "What I had with Jessica is over."

"Are you sure it's not just a couple's fight?"

"No. What she wants for me it's not something I can give her. She wants my full attention all the time, and she's constantly worried about everything."

"Maybe it's because she loves you."

"Yes, and I love her, too, but it's not going to last long-term. I need my space to pursue things I care about, but she doesn't understand."

"So, are you definitely breaking up with her?"

"It's over. We talked over lunch and agreed it's the best for both." His intense gaze was looking for a reaction. "But I have feelings for you."

She nervously giggled and stroked his arm. "I have feelings for you, too. Since Josh took me to the café and I saw you after all those years, my heart stopped, but when I learned you were engaged, it was like having an ice bucket poured over my head."

"I have to say that I was shocked by your beauty that day."

"I know. Remember spilling your coffee when trying to stand up?"

"What an awkward moment. You must have thought I was dumb."

"Can't deny that it was amusing, but I recognized you from when we were teens. Let's stop talking now. How about an appetizer before dinner?" Rachel kissed him passionately.

"I'm sure dinner can wait."

They began a twirling motion of kissing and taking off clothes. Their bodies were perfectly fit for each other in a love game that seemed to have no end. Exhausted from the lovemaking, they cuddled for some time afterward.

Exhausted from the lovemaking, they cuddled for some time afterward.

"Do you still want to cook dinner?" Matt held Rachel by the shoulder while her head was resting on his chest.

"*Mmm,*" she exhaled. "The appetizer was fantastic. Can we have seconds?"

"Glad you asked." Matt softly rolled over her and begun a new round of touching and kissing. No part of their bodies was left unexplored, sometimes with smooth moves and other times with blasts of energy. It was late that night when they decided to order some sushi.

IN A DIFFERENT part of town, another event would also help shape Matt and Jessica's future forever. Josh rang the bell at the Daltons' mansion, and Jessica came to receive him. She was wearing a tartan pleated miniskirt with a solid pink top and a simple ruby pendant. She had her hair arranged in a casually twisted low bun that made her look neat and cute.

Josh froze with his mouth open for a few seconds. "You look fabulous." It was the only thing he could say.

"Thank you." Jessica's eyes beamed, and Josh blushed. "Please come in."

They went into the living area where John was having a drink. "Hi, Josh. Thanks for coming. Would you care for a drink?"

"Hello, John. Thank you. I think I may need one."

John laughed and guided him by the shoulder to the bar area. "C'mon, you don't have to be nervous. How long has it been since we saw you last time in this house?" And without waiting for a response, he continued, "Let me think. I guess since graduating from high school?"

At that time, Mary Dalton came to the room. "*Josh*. Nice seeing you again. Are you staying for dinner?"

Josh felt overwhelmed by the show of kindness. "I appreciate the invitation, Mary, but…."

"No excuses, Josh. We would love to have you

join us tonight." The firmness of Mary's words and the look of Jessica's eyes did the trick.

"Okay, Mary. I'd be happy to stay."

"Wonderful," John interrupted. "But first, you and I have to have a little talk. Let's take our drinks and go to the study."

Both men left the room, and Mary looked excitedly at her daughter. "Josh is very handsome and seems to be the same nice person he was when you dated in high school. Did you say he's a lawyer also?"

"Yes, Mom. He's very nice, and we've been friends since high school. We went to different law schools but always kept in touch. We're good friends."

"Are you sure just friends? I see how he looks at you."

Now it was Jessica's turn to blush. "*Mom.* Don't start with your match-making games."

"Why? You said that your relationship with Matt is over. I think Josh is a much better choice."

Jessica shook her head but smiled as she followed her mother to the kitchen. When dinner was ready, they all got together at the table.

"I have an announcement to make." John raised his glass while Josh grinned. "Mr. Josh Miller has accepted to join the new Dalton, Miller and Associates law firm. Here's to a successful partnership."

Jessica proudly smiled and put her hand on

Josh's shoulder while Mary nodded in approval. "Congratulations, Josh."

They spent the rest of the evening talking about Josh's past and developing plans for the new firm. Josh had made an excellent impression at the Daltons'. When he was ready to leave, Jessica went with him to the door.

"Thank you, Jessica, for the opportunity to talk to your father. Without you, this wouldn't have happened."

"I think it's great. We've known each other for a long time and thinking about working together is exciting."

"Can I ask you something?" Josh bit his lip while looking at her.

"Don't scare me. You look so serious." Her grin was inviting him to ask whatever he wanted.

"It's about Matt." He mumbled. "Are you still in love with him? What is going on in your relationship?"

She exhaled. "It's still very recent, but the answer is that I've been disappointed and don't see the relationship going anywhere. I'm certain we don't have a future together, and I've already discussed it with Matt."

His eyes brightened. "That's great." And realizing what he just said, he held up his hands. "Oh, sorry, I didn't mean it the way that came out."

"Don't worry." She took his hands. "I know how you feel. Let's go slowly." Jessica gave him a sweet kiss on his cheek. "We'll spend a lot of time together, *partner*." And she went back into the house.

Josh never saw so many stars in the sky or felt the breeze being so enjoyable. For him, it was a beautiful night despite the frantic dance of the tree branches choreographed by the strong wind and people running around for cover from the freezing temperatures.

Chapter 26

"RACHEL? THIS IS Tyler. Just checking to see how things are going with Jessica and Matt." "Wonderful. I confirmed that they broke up, and I'm already seeing Matt."

"Wow. You're fast. I'm free to make a move on Jessica then." He couldn't contain his excitement.

"Better do. I heard that you're not the only one interested in her."

"What?" Tyler replied in a subdued voice.

"It looks like Josh is trying to revive their flame from high school. Maybe you need to talk to Mrs. Dalton, who you know well, and find out what's going on."

"I surely will." He hung up and called Mary Dalton.

"Good morning, Mary; this is Tyler."

"Oh. Hi, Tyler. What can I do for you?"

"We talked a few days ago about your daughter's

relationship with Matt and the need to do something about it."

"Yes, but fortunately, that's not a problem anymore. Jessica decided to break up with him, and last night we had a delightful dinner with Josh Miller. He'll become a partner in the new practice my husband is starting with Jessica, and it looks like he has his eyes on Jessica."

"She can't do this to me." His voice started off sharp, and then he broke down.

"Sorry, Tyler, but I can't manage Jessica's heart. You better accept that she sees you only as a friend."

RACHEL LEFT A message on Matt's phone that he read during the lunch break. THE DEA AGENT CALLED, SAYING THAT THEY ARE GOING TO SERVE THE SEARCH WARRANT FOR THE BREWERY LAB TODAY.

Matt's pulse accelerated. "Rachel, is it happening today?"

"Yes, it may already have happened. We're getting to the end."

The rest of the afternoon was unbearable. Every minute seemed to last an eternity. Matt finished his school day and went to see Rachel, hoping that her company would help control his anxiety. It was around five when the phone rang, and Rachel put it on speaker.

"Mrs. Avila, I'm calling from the DEA. As presenter of the accusation against DB Corp., I'm giving you an update. We searched the brewery lab and didn't find anything out of the ordinary or suspicious."

"What?" Matt raised his voice. "How could that be?"

"We inspected the facilities and especially the research lab as suggested, and it's a first-class operation. Clean as a whistle."

"It's impossible. There must be something." Matt's breathing quickened, and his face turned pale.

"I would suggest that you cease with this ghost chasing. An official of the company mentioned that you were harassing them on some water compliance issue and then with this conspiracy theory about threats and violence. They may go after you in civil court. There is nothing else we can do." The agent hung up, and they were left looking at each other perplexed and beaten.

Matt was still shaking his head. "There has to be an explanation."

"Maybe they were involved in some illegal business at the time of the fire but not now?" Rachel tried to find an answer.

"But why would they be so worried about our investigation? We know the threats and violence were real."

They kept searching their brains for something that could explain why the DEA didn't find anything when Matt's phone rang.

"Matt? This is Mario Ramirez. You told me to call if we saw something unusual."

"Yes, Mario. Did you guys see anything?"

"There was a DEA inspection today."

"We know Mario, but they didn't find anything unusual at the lab."

"Because they moved everything out."

Matt jumped from his seat. "What did you say?"

"Our guys have seen movement around that lab in the last couple of days. Boxes being moved into vans leaving the brewery."

"That's why the DEA didn't find anything." Matt was pacing around the room, gesturing.

"But knowing this doesn't help us. The authorities will think it's another part of our conspiracy theory." Rachel put her palms down, trying to control her excitement.

"But we know." Mario's voice came through the speaker loud and clear.

"What do you know?" Rachel had her eyes wide open, staring at the phone.

"Our guys inside the brewery detected the loading of boxes, and another group of friends followed the vans. They went to a warehouse in Blue River. We didn't call you before because we were trying to complete the picture."

"You did great, Mario. We love you guys," Matt shouted.

"Please send us the address of the warehouse." Rachel rubbed her hands together.

They immediately called the DEA agent and provided the information gathered by the brewery operators and their friends.

"Mr. Hernandez. Is this another figment of your imagination? You put me in a bad position with the judge when we didn't find anything, and are you suggesting that I go again for a warrant to search a warehouse in a small town?"

"I know we've been accused of creating a conspiracy theory and didn't provide any strong evidence, but this would be it. Why would they move boxes from that lab into a warehouse? It's not just me, but we have witnesses working at the brewery that you can talk to."

"Okay. Let me see what I can do."

Don Brackman went to see Frank at his office.

"Good morning, Don. Visiting me on a Saturday? Everything under control?"

"Yes." Don walked with firm strides and sat across Frank. "We had an inspection from the DEA yesterday."

Frank's eyes went wide, but he continued.

"Of course, they didn't find anything and left with apologies."

"*Bravo*. Good job, Don. Let's hope that *Mr. Hernandez* stops nosing around now. I know it's the morning, but this deserves a drink." Frank got up and took two glasses and a bottle of cognac from a cabinet.

They continued chatting and laughing about the police getting out of the lab, embarrassed and without anything to show for their efforts.

"Can you imagine Matt's face when they told him the results of the search? I would have paid to be there." Frank was shaking with laughter.

THREE DAYS LATER, police officers walked into DB Corp. headquarters, arrested Don Brackman, and took files and computers. The employees couldn't understand why their boss was cuffed and escorted to a patrol car until later in the day when they saw reporter, Rachel Avila, describing a news alert.

A COMBINED INVESTIGATION BY THE DEA AND LOCAL LAW ENFORCEMENT AGENCIES SUCCESSFULLY DISMANTLED A DRUG TRAFFICKING HUB HIDDEN AS A RESEARCH LABORATORY AT THE LOCAL BREWERY. THE HEAD OF DB CORP. HAS BEEN ARRESTED AND

CHARGED AS ONE OF THE BRAINS OF THE ILLEGAL OPERATION.

On the next day, another team of four agents went to the legal offices of Frank Morris. They showed up at his office while Frank was reviewing a report with his assistant.

"Mr. Frank Morris?" The leading officer looked at him with a distinctive, authoritative voice.

"Yes." Frank squinted his eyes.

"I'm a DEA agent, and these officers are from the local police department. You're being charged with money laundering and participation in drug trafficking. You need to come with us."

"This has to be a mistake," Frank mumbled.

"Your partner, Don Brackman, has been arrested, and we found documentation that shows your association with him to produce illegal substances under cover of the brewery research laboratory. There is also evidence of money laundering through DB Corp. and your legal firm."

"That's not true. I'm just DB Corp.'s lawyer and don't know anything about drug trafficking."

"Mr. Morris. Don't you own the Green Acres farm near San Diego?"

"Yes. I see that you've done your homework, agent," Frank sneered.

"Then maybe you can explain how hops bales with shipping labels from your farm ended up at the warehouse we raided, where we found the drug-producing equipment."

"I have a side agricultural business that supplies hops to the brewery."

"We found heroin and coca paste inside those bales."

"Those idiots," Frank muttered.

The police read him his rights and took him into custody.

"Dad, are you also going to be charged for being Frank's partner?"

"Don't worry, Jessica. I already talked to the police, and they understand that I was not aware of Frank's wrongdoings. There are also internal memos where I pointed out overbilling that Frank never addressed."

"I don't understand how Frank was dragged into that business." Jessica shook her head.

"He was a lawyer among the many trying to make a living in the San Diego area. At some point in time, he successfully defended some drug dealers and met more of them. They belonged to the same cartel doing business with Brackman. The turning point in his career was when the brewery lab caught fire. He developed a successful defense based on buying influences and witnesses, and Don Brackman got an eye on him, making Frank the lead attorney for his corporation. That was not enough for Frank. In his quest to become a millionaire, he proposed to channel some of the money launderings through his legal practice."

Jessica couldn't take her gaze away from his father. "And how did you get involved with him?"

"He wanted to expand into this part of the country and proposed I become his partner. We knew each other from law school, but, of course, I didn't know how he had become so successful. Creating a partnership with someone having a portfolio that included DB Corp. seemed to be a great opportunity, and I took it."

"And you never suspected anything?"

"He kept the relationship with Don Brackman close to his chest, and I only knew that DB Corp. was our largest client, so I tried to help as needed to keep our main client happy. However, I noticed some suspicious billings for large amounts that, as I said, I brought to Frank's attention without answers. That's why I decided to end the partnership last week."

John turned toward the office door. "And here comes our partner partly responsible for the investigation that ended that drug trafficking operation."

Josh grinned and sat next to Jessica. "Thanks. However, I have to say that Matt was the key player in pursuing the case."

"Don't be modest, Josh." Jessica crossed her arms

and tilted her head. "We know you've been active in talking to the police and searching for witnesses."

"That's true," John intervened. "But let's talk about our partnership. I suspect some clients who were part of Frank's portfolio will contact me now. So, we may have a busy start-up to our new venture."

"Yes, Dad." Jessica chuckled. "But let's make sure we don't take *all* of his clients."

A burst of laughter followed, and John nodded. "We certainly know better."

"If you'll excuse me, I would like to make a call. I want to know how Tyler is taking all this. I don't think he knew anything about his father's businesses." Jessica got up and left the office.

"HI TYLER, THIS is Jessica."

"Hello, Jessica. How're you doing?" The sad tone of his voice echoed the turmoil fogging his mind.

"Fine, but I wanted to know how you're taking all the news about DB Corp. and your father."

"It's a shock," he muttered. "I knew he had a close relationship with Brackman, but I thought it was just trying to please a large client. I asked about some things that looked strange lately, but he wouldn't share, saying that he wanted to protect me. I see the meaning now."

"I'm sorry it happened this way. What are you planning to do?"

"You don't need to be sorry. My father got himself into it, and now he'll pay with ten or more years in prison. It's still hard to believe."

"Any way we can help?" Jessica sounded genuinely sympathetic.

"Thanks, but there's nothing you can do. I know you broke up with Matt, and now you will try to move on and maybe building a relationship with Josh."

"It's too early to tell, but it may go that way."

"You deserve to be happy, Jessica, and Josh seems to be a great guy. I'm planning to go back to New York and restart my life there."

"Good luck, Tyler. You know that you have me, my parents, and Josh here if you need anything." Jessica hung up and blew out her cheeks.

A COUPLE OF weeks later, Matt rang the bell at Rachel's apartment.

"Is the most famous reporter ready to go?" He presented a flower bouquet that she smelled and received with an ear-to-ear smile.

"Just adding the finishing touches." She put the flowers in a vase. "Is Josh going also?"

"Yes, and he's taking Jessica with him."

"Wow. Is their relationship serious now?"

"It looks like that. I'm glad for them both. After I broke up with Jessica, they've been getting closer."

"Are you sure about your feelings?" Rachel had a tight-lipped smile.

Matt got closer and pulled her body toward his. "I'm glad we're still friends with her and Josh, but I'm thrilled I have you." And he gave her a passionate kiss.

"Okay." Her misty eyes looked into his. "We better go now, or we're going to be late."

Matt laughed. "You're right. However, I would love to be late."

"Behave, Mr. Hernandez. Those people are waiting for the guys who solved the brewery fire mystery." She pushed him gently and picked up her purse.

THE AFTERNOON WAS pleasant, and about fifteen people gathered around a table improvised with a board put over a couple of sawhorses on Mario Ramirez's daughter's patio. Everybody began clapping when Matt, Rachel, Josh, and Jessica arrived.

"Come, friends. This is your home." Mario hugged them.

"We wouldn't miss this opportunity. We've heard

great things about Latino parties." Matt grinned. "This is my girlfriend, Rachel."

Mario's daughter shouted, "The Channel 5 reporter."

Mario smiled while Rachel blushed.

"And this is Jessica." He paused to look at her and Josh and winked. "They say they are friends, but we think there is something else going on."

Everybody began shouting "kiss…kiss" while clapping. Jessica seemed to burn Matt with her gaze but quickly smiled after Josh planted a kiss on her mouth and all howled and whistled.

"It's a great start." Josh was on cloud nine.

"And the best to come," Mario added, "music, dancing, and great food brought by my cousin from his restaurant."

Matt tilted his head. "Isn't that the restaurant by Blue River we went through the last time we were here?"

"Yes, but don't worry. He didn't prepare his *special* tacos for us." Mario roared, and everybody was shaking and roaring with laughter.

Turtle Creek
Enigma of the Trail

Ruben Elustondo

"The storyline was exciting from the beginning to the end. I couldn't put the book down. Highly suggest reading it"

- Amazon review.

WHEN THE LIFELESS body of a young athlete is found near the forest trail with signs of a violent struggle, the people of the peaceful Turtle Creek village are in shock. The police investigation will be under scrutiny when the governor's son, David, is identified as a suspect and the case is quickly dragged into the political arena.

The governor's husband, a famous doctor and director of an upscale clinic is engaged in a flirtatious relationship with an attractive young woman who works with him and manipulates the relation to cover up her criminal activities.

A couple of schoolmates of the victim volunteer some information that further complicates the situation of David, but their story is not clean and will soon backfire on them. After a shrewd private investigator provides new evidence in favor of the suspect's claim of innocence, the investigation seems to get nowhere and the prosecutor feels like reaching a dead end.

A routine follow-up on a couple of potential witnesses and the death of a new suspect will provide the leads to solve the mysterious crime. However, an obscure character who monitors the situation from a distance will play a leading role in the unexpected end.

Made in the USA
Columbia, SC
20 June 2021

40253142R00167